#0

The Baseball Thief

THE MITCHELL  BROTHERS SERIES

#8
The Baseball Thief

THE MITCHELL BROTHERS SERIES

Brian McFarlane

Fenn Publishing Company Ltd.
Bolton, Canada

THE BASEBALL THIEF
BOOK EIGHT IN THE MITCHELL BROTHERS SERIES
A Fenn Publishing Book / May 2005

Copyright 2005 © Brian McFarlane

Fenn Publishing Company Ltd.
Bolton, Ontario, Canada

Distributed in Canada by H.B. Fenn and Company Ltd.
Bolton, Ontario, Canada, L7E 1W2
www.hbfenn.com

Library and Archives Canada Cataloguing in Publication

McFarlane, Brian, 1931-
        Baseball thief / Brian McFarlane.

(Mitchell Brothers series ; 8)
For ages 8–12.
ISBN 1-55168-276-1

        I. Title. II. Series: McFarlane, Brian, 1931- Mitchell
brothers series ; 8.

PS8575.F37B38 2005   jC813'.54   C2005-902377-5

THE BASEBALL THIEF

NOTE FROM THE AUTHOR

When the Mitchell brothers were growing up in the 1930s, no black players were allowed to play major league baseball. They were called coloured players then. This ban applied to one of the greatest pitchers in the history of the game—Leroy "Satchel" Paige. When infielder Jackie Robinson finally broke the barriers of discrimination in 1947, after signing with the Brooklyn Dodgers, Satchel Paige was close to 40 years old. Despite his advanced age, manager Bill Veeck of the Cleveland Indians brought him to the American League in 1948 as the oldest rookie ever to play major league ball. Twelve years after making his debut, closing out a Hall of Fame career, he appeared in three innings for the Kansas City Athletics to become the oldest man to pitch in a major league game. He was 59.

Our story finds Satchel during his barnstorming days, when his touring All Star team travels to the North Country for a series of exhibition games against local clubs. Satchel's chance encounter with the Mitchell brothers, Max and Marty, leads to some surprising events on and off the ball diamond.

Brian McFarlane

CHAPTER 1

SATCHEL COMES TO TOWN

"Come on, Marty! Put down that Hardy Boys book. Grab your catcher's mitt. And find your bike. I want to get down to the ballpark early," Max Mitchell shouted through the screen door to his younger brother. "First game in the weekend tournament starts at six o'clock."

Marty leaped up from the sofa, threw down the book he was reading, found his mitt and rushed outside. It took him a few minutes to find his bike because he'd put it away in the shed—something he rarely did.

Marty emerged from the shadows of the shed with his bike. "I can't believe it was there," he said, giggling. "Last place I would have thought to look."

The brothers wore their baseball uniforms— white with red trim. The name MILLERS splashed across the chest. Their ball gloves were stashed in the carrier on Max's new bike—a CCM Glider.

1

"Sorry, Max," Marty said. "I lost track of time. Happens every time I read a Hardy Boys book."

"Which one you reading now?" Max asked.

"*The Secret of the Old Mill.* I was at the part where a kid falls into the rapids. He's about to be smashed into the jagged rocks. The Hardy Boys are trying to save him. They could be smashed to pieces, too."

"Do you think they will?"

"How do I know? I had to put the book down when you called."

Max chuckled. "I'm sure they'll survive. And they'll rescue the kid. I'd bet my shirt they do."

"I get it. You've read that book."

"No I haven't," Max replied. "But if they don't save the kid and they all get smashed to smithereens on the rocks, guess what?"

"What?"

"That's the end of the Hardy Boys. They'll be food for the fishes. Don't worry. They'll drag the kid out. If they don't, the last book in the series will be called *The Hardy Boys Funeral.*"

"Gee, I hope not," mutter Marty. "I love those books. Frank and Joe Hardy lead exciting lives."

"Not like us," Max said, mounting his bike. "We're just normal kids from the North Country. Nothing exciting ever happens to us."

Max started off down Centre Street, pedalling hard. He was 17, a handsome six-footer with blond hair and blue eyes. His red-haired brother was two inches shorter and two years younger. Max was a pitcher, Marty a catcher.

"Hey! Wait up!" Marty shouted, scrambling to catch up. "I want to tell you a baseball joke."

Max rolled his eyes. "Okay, but just one."

Marty said, "Why did the coach kick Cinderella off the baseball team?"

Max said, "I give up."

Marty giggled. "Because she ran away from the ball."

Max grunted. "I'll give you a three out of ten for that one," he said.

At Main Street, Max turned right and coasted down the hill leading into town. Marty was close behind.

The Gray paper mill was off to their left and the shift was changing. Men in work clothes—clothes covered with sawdust—walked down one side of the street. One of them shouted, "Hey, Max! You pitching tonight?"

Max nodded and grinned at the man, who gave him a thumbs up.

"And I'm catching," Marty shouted as he sped by. "I plan on hitting a couple of homers. Better get there early."

"Your next homer will be your first, kid," the man said, laughing.

Suddenly, Max heard a loud noise.

Beep! Beeeep!

He looked over his shoulder and gasped.

"What is it?" Marty cried.

"A bus! An old school bus. And it's coming fast! It's out of control!" Max called back. "Get out of the way. It's all over the road."

"We can't get out of the way," Marty hollered. "The road's too narrow and there are big ditches on either side."

The driver of the bus was wrestling with the wheel and pounding on the horn.

Beep! Beep! Beep!

"Faster!" shouted Max.

Max and Marty pedalled faster. The bus was gaining on them. The hill began to level off. Shops appeared on either side. The town's only grocery store was just ahead. It was payday and business at the store was brisk. Customers milled about out front, oblivious to the danger.

"My gosh!" Marty pointed. "There's the widow Anderson. And she's about to cross the street."

"I'll warn her about the bus!" Max cried out, pedalling even faster. "Mrs. Anderson! Mrs. Anderson! Look out! A runaway bus is coming down the hill."

Mrs. Anderson was hard of hearing. She plodded on, then stopped, looked around and cupped a hand to one ear.

"Mrs. Anderson!" Max shrieked. "Look out!"

Startled, Mrs. Anderson had stopped midway across the street. She was pulling a boy's wagon full of groceries. She looked up and froze when she heard Max. Then she saw the yellow bus hurtling toward her. She tried to scurry to safety, but her foot caught in a pothole. Down she went— flat on her face. Then she screamed.

Max braked to a stop, leaped off his bike and raced to help Mrs. Anderson.

"Twisted my ankle," she murmured. "And my head hurts. Can't get up…"

Beep! Beep! Beeeep!!!!

Max gripped her under both arms and scooped her up off the pavement. In two strides he carried her to safety. But he couldn't save his bike. A split second later, the wheels of the bus flattened the frame and left the wheels and handlebars a twisted mess.

"Oh, no!" cried Max.

The bus roared past. Max heard the driver shout, "No brakes! Can't stop!" As people hurried to get out of the way, cars on the street swerved close to the curb. The bus, now on more even ground, began to slow down. It rumbled on for 100 yards or more, and then coasted to a stop next to the ball field.

The driver jumped out of the open door and ran back to where Max was attending to Mrs. Anderson.

"Oh, no!" he gasped, his face clearly indicating his dread.

Mrs. Anderson lay on the ground. The bus had crushed her wagon full of groceries. Broken eggs, spilled milk and smashed vegetables lay all around.

A crowd of people came running to help. "Is she all right, Max?" someone asked.

"I think so. Just frightened. Look! She's coming to."

Mrs. Anderson's eyelids fluttered, then her eyes opened wide. She found herself looking into the face of the bus driver, who stared down at her, deeply concerned.

The bus driver squeezed out a huge sigh of relief. But Mrs. Anderson choked back a scream. The man staring down at her was like no one she'd ever seen before in Indian River. His face was as brown as a chocolate Easter egg.

CHAPTER 2

THE SHERIFF ARRIVES

Sheriff Doug "Dugie" Dugan arrived on the scene. His teenage son Darrel was with him. Darrel was a ballplayer. He played the infield and pitched for the Millers. Darrel and his father had been on their way to the ballpark when the sheriff heard people screaming. He rushed to the scene of the accident and quickly took charge. He shouldered the bus driver aside and began to help Mrs. Anderson to her feet.

"You'll be all right, ma'am," he said. "Just a little shook up. But I'm afraid your groceries are ruined."

"I'll be glad to pay for them," the bus driver said. He leaned toward Mrs. Anderson. "I'm so sorry, ma'am. The brakes failed and…"

"Quiet, you," ordered the sheriff. He glowered at the stranger. "I'll deal with you in a minute."

Darrel handed something to his dad. "Here's her purse," he said. Then he whistled. "Who-wee. There's a lot of money inside."

"Darrel, nobody asked you to look inside," he said gruffly. "Give it here."

Max pushed forward. "Don't you think we'd better call for an ambulance, Sheriff Dugan? Mrs. Anderson hit her head. She may have a concussion. And her ankle is badly twisted. It may be broken. I don't think you should lift her. Just in case, sir."

Sheriff Dugan had been prepared to carry Mrs. Anderson to his police cruiser and drive her home. Perhaps give her an aspirin or two. He hadn't considered taking her to the hospital. The victim didn't look seriously injured. Still, the Mitchell kid had a point. And Mrs. Anderson was moaning in pain.

"You're right, kid," the sheriff mumbled. "The old lady should go to the hospital. Just in case." He cocked his head. "No need to call the ambulance. Somebody called for one. It's on its way. I can hear the siren."

Sheriff Dugan was a tall man with a florid face and a southern accent. He had moved to Indian River two years earlier, in 1934, when the former sheriff had retired. He often talked about his "southern roots" and seemed to regret his decision to settle in the North. "Too much darned snow in winter," he once complained to Harry Mitchell, owner and editor of the *Indian River Review* and the father of the Mitchell brothers. "And the summers are too short. But here I don't have to worry about them people," he grumbled, without elaborating on who "them people" were.

The ambulance attendants carefully hoisted Mrs. Anderson onto a stretcher and slid it smoothly into the back of the ambulance. The ambulance roared off, siren blaring. Meanwhile, the sheriff took notes and asked more questions. He even spoke briefly with two or three of the ball players who had left the bus and were standing quietly in the background. His lanky son stood next to him, chewing gum, ball glove in hand.

Max walked over to Darrel.

"Hey, Darrel. Some day, huh? I thought Marty and I were roadkill for sure. And Mrs. Anderson, too."

Darrel nodded and told Max about the old lady's purse.

"I peeked inside and she had a wad of bills in there. At least 100 dollars."

"No way!" said Max. "I always thought Mrs. Anderson was poor."

"So did I," Darrel said. "She sure acts like she's poor. Wears the same dress almost every day. Won't buy candy for the kids on Halloween. Drags her groceries home in a squeaky old wagon."

Sheriff Dugan began questioning the bus driver.

"See yer license," he said curtly. When the man fished a driver's license out of his wallet and handed it over, the sheriff clucked his tongue.

"A Louisiana license," he said. "We don't see many of those up here. What's this name I see on it? Leroy Paige?"

"That's right, sir, Leroy Paige," he said in a lazy drawl. "My friends call me Satchel. You a baseball fan you may have heard of me. Satchel Paige."

"Can't say that I have," said the sheriff.

But Max felt a surge of excitement. He had heard the name Satchel Paige.

"I'm not a ball fan," the sheriff said, "although my son plays on the local team. My only interest is law and order. And you've just broken the law, mister. Driving dangerously. You nearly killed that old woman."

"But the brakes failed on the team bus," Satchel Paige argued. "Wasn't a thing I could do about it." He nodded toward Max. "Thanks to this young man the lady wasn't run over. And I'll gladly pay for her groceries that got ruint. And I'll pay for the young man's broken bike, too."

He pulled a pair of 20 bills from his pocket and showed them to the sheriff.

Sheriff Dugan recoiled. "Boy, you waving money in my face. You tryin' to bribe me?"

"No, sir, I'd never do that."

"But you just did. Yessir, you are so trying to bribe me. That's another serious breach of the law. You better come with me. You're under arrest. You are in deep trouble, boy. You may be facing a few days in jail."

Max leaped to his feet. "Sheriff, I don't think you understand. You're not looking at the facts. This man can't be blamed if the brakes on the bus failed. And he wasn't bribing you. He meant the money to cover Mrs. Anderson's grocery bill. And my bicycle."

"Quiet, Mitchell," the sheriff ordered. "You got a law degree, let's see it. Otherwise, stop tryin' to tell me how to run my business."

"Sheriff Dugan, it's just that..."

Darrel Dugan stepped forward. "Max, I saw it all. This old darkie was trying to bribe my dad. I'm a witness."

Max turned to his friend, shocked at the way he almost sneered when he used the word "darkie." There was a look of contempt on Darrel's face.

Max felt a tug on his sleeve. He turned to see his father, owner and editor of the *Indian River Review*, at his side.

"Tell me what happened here, son," Harry Mitchell said. "I saw the commotion from my office window. I was the one who called the ambulance."

Both Max and Marty took turns explaining what had happened.

"It seems the brakes failed on an old bus carrying a touring ball team," Max said. "The bus went out of control coming down the hill."

"If it wasn't for Max, the bus would have run over poor Mrs. Anderson," Marty chimed in. "Max saved her life but it cost him his new bike. And the bus driver—the Negro man over there—wanted to give her some money for the groceries. The stupid sheriff called it a bribe."

"And now Mr. Paige is going to jail," Max added. "It just doesn't seem fair."

"It may not be fair," said his father. "Remember, some folks have little tolerance for people who don't look and think like them. I'll go talk to him. See what I can do. You fellows run along to the ballpark. I'll see you there later."

"Okay, Dad. But there's one more thing."

"There is? What is it?"

"Dad, don't you recognize the name—Satchel Paige? I've read all about him. He's probably the greatest Negro pitcher in baseball. And he's right here in Indian River."

"Yeah. And they're about to throw him in jail," Marty snorted.

"Satchel Paige!" Harry Mitchell said in surprise. "I heard he was coming to the North Country, leading a team of coloured ballplayers on a barnstorming tour. They're scheduled to play here in Indian River in a couple of weeks. I better rush over to the jail. Looks like Satchel and his teammates may have to reschedule some ball games. They may be in town for a few days."

12

At the ballpark, the Millers warmed up for their game against Chatsworth. The infielders fielded ground balls, the outfielders shagged flies and the fans made their way to seats in the stands. One of them shouted at Max. "Where's your dad? He's still the manager, isn't he?"

Max laughed and said, "Yep. He hasn't given up on us yet."

Max threw a dozen warmup pitches to Marty along the sidelines, then nodded and said, "That's enough. I'm ready." By then their father was standing behind the team bench. And Satchel Paige was with him.

"Here's the story," their father said when Max and Marty rushed over and shook Satchel's big hand. "Mr. Paige has been released—temporarily. The sheriff placed him in my custody. His team can't leave town until there's a hearing. And we learn the extent of Mrs. Anderson's injuries. So Satchel and his catcher, Josh Gibson, are coming to stay at our house tonight. I wish we had room for the other members of the team but we don't."

Satchel grinned and said, "Not to worry, Mr. Mitchell. The other players are younger than Josh and me. They don't mind sleeping on the team bus. They have blankets and pillows on board."

"What about the brakes on the bus?" Marty asked. "Can they be fixed?"

"Not right away," said his father. "I had a mechanic take a quick look at them. He thinks they may have been tampered with. Could that be, Satch?"

"Maybe. In the last town we played in, a couple of dudes didn't like us much. They had a chance to mess with the brakes while we was playing ball. But we've got no proof."

Harry grimaced. "Well, my mechanic has to order some parts from the city," he said. "The bus can stay where it is—right over there by the ballpark—until the parts arrive. But it may be a few days before they get here."

Satchel nodded. "That'll be okay. We're used to setbacks." He turned to Max and said, "I saw you throwing. You've got a nice motion, a good fastball. You mind if I offer you a few words of advice?"

"I'd love your advice," Max answered. "Anything to make me a better pitcher. Dad's the manager but he's never been a pitcher."

"That's true," admitted Mr. Mitchell. "I don't know a whole lot about the fundamentals of pitching."

"Let's you and me wander off a ways," Satchel said. "Have a nice talk. I want to see how you grip the ball. And I've got some thoughts on your dee-livery."

14

Satchel and Max huddled next to the grandstand. Max listened eagerly to the words of wisdom that rolled off Satchel's tongue. He absorbed the tips on pitching: the best way to grip the ball, how to deliver it and follow through, how to pick a runner off base and how to field a bunt.

He couldn't wait to face the Chatsworth Cougars. When the umpire cried, "Play ball!" he headed to the mound with a big smile on his face. He thought: *I'm the luckiest ballplayer in the world. I've just heard an amazing lecture on pitching from a master of the art. Now I'll have to see if I remember his tips when I start throwing them in to Marty.*

His first three pitches had the leadoff batter swinging wildly. He struck out and headed back to the bench, grumbling to himself.

Marty chuckled. "Great start, Max!" he shouted. "They're not going to touch you today."

CHAPTER 3
THE HOUSE GUESTS

Amy Mitchell had never had two Negro gentlemen in her house for dinner before. *And it's not surprising*, she thought, *there aren't any coloured folks living in Indian River. Not one family.*

They all sat down to dinner, with Big Fella, the Mitchell's prize husky, sleeping at their feet, and they talked about the game.

"Chatsworth has some fine players," Josh Gibson said. "Some good amateurs. Their pitcher—Goose Goslin—showed me a good curveball. But you mowed them down with your fastball, Max. What did they get—two hits?"

Marty blurted, "That's what I got all by myself—two hits. And one of them a homer."

"The Millers won three to one, which is the important thing," Harry Mitchell said. "We don't want any swelled heads in this family. Still, congratulations are in order. You boys played well."

"Thanks, Dad," Max said. "Mr. Paige—Satchel—gave me some pointers that really helped. We should beat Storm Valley tomorrow. And if the Cougars beat Grafton, we'll face the Cougars again in the championship game on Sunday."

"Satchel and Josh," Marty began, only to be interrupted by his mother.

"It's Mr. Paige and Mr. Gibson, son," she said quietly. "Remember your manners."

"No, Mom," Marty replied. "Normally I'd call them that. But they insist on being called Satchel and Josh. That's what everybody calls them."

"That's right, Mrs. Mitchell," Satchel confirmed. "Even the bat boys call us that."

Amy Mitchell smiled. "Then I guess it's all right," she said, as she poured milk into glasses.

Marty picked up the conversation. "Satchel and Josh, since you're going to be here for the weekend, maybe you can help Dad with the team," he suggested. "Be like assistant coaches or something."

"We both love working with young players," Josh said. "If you don't mind, Harry?"

"Mind? I can use all the help I can get," Harry Mitchell said. "Satch has already helped Max. You men can probably teach our kids a lot in a couple of days."

"Now that that's settled, let's forget the tournament for now," Marty suggested. "Max and I want to hear about Josh Gibson and Satchel Paige. How'd you fellows get to be ballplayers?"

"I'll let Satch do most of the talking," Josh Gibson said. "He's as good at that as he is at pitching."

Satchel wiped his mouth with a napkin and said, "I'm a talker, all right. Josh don't like to talk about himself. But he's one of the greatest hitters—and best catchers—I've ever seen." Satchel turned to Marty. "If you're smart, son, you'll get Josh out in the backyard before the sun goes down. He'll teach you more tricks about catching and hitting a baseball than you ever thought existed."

"I'd love that," Marty said, his eyes bright. He glanced at the clock on the wall. "But there's lots of time before sundown. And I want to hear all about you, Satchel. How you got into baseball."

Satchel grinned. "Well, I grew up in a little wood shack in Mobile, Alabama. That's a long way south from here. My mommy and daddy raised 11 children in that shack. I was number seven.

"I was like every other kid in those day, running around in hand-me-down clothes, lucky to have a torn shirt to wear. Shoes? I can't remember having shoes.

"We threw a lot of rocks when I was a kid. We'd play in the dirt and hit rocks with a stick. And we'd run around in the dirt, sliding into bases we made out of cardboard. Then we'd go down to the bay to wash the dirt off. The bay is where the white folks lived. They owned the land. They'd threaten to shoot us if we trespassed."

"Shoot you?" Marty said, his eyes wide. "Just for trespassing? Are you serious?"

"One of my brothers came home one day with some buckshot in his bum," Josh said, smiling.

"With 11 kids in the family, I'll bet you never had enough to eat," Marty said solemnly.

Satchel chuckled. "By gosh we did. Just enough. My mommy was strict. She made us all get jobs and bring in money for food. I collected empty pop bottles and turned them in for a few pennies. Then, when I was about ten years old, I got a job carrying satchels down at the railroad depot. People laughed because I could carry so many satchels they couldn't see me under all those bags. Pretty soon my buddies began calling me 'Satchel' and the name stuck. Didn't get called Leroy very often after that."

"But you haven't told us how you got into baseball," Marty urged.

"Son, I'm getting to that. I got a job at the ballpark one summer, sweeping out the stands. And I saw those pro ballplayers throwing the ball around. Heck, I could throw apples faster than that. And with a lot more control. The white boys used to hurl apples at us coming home from school and I hurled them right back. A lot of those white boys cried for their mommies when I cracked them with a rotten apple. Then their mommies would run after me and yell, 'Get on home, black boy!' It got so I hated those words.

"By the time I was a teenager I was hurling baseballs like they were bullets. I made a team and the coach put me in the outfield 'cause I could throw and I could hit. One day an opposing team knocked two of our pitchers out of the game in the first inning and the coach called on me. I was all gawky, arms and legs flailing in all directions. But my pitches must have looked like mothballs 'cause I struck out 16 straight batters. Didn't give up a hit. Man, that felt good. I told the coach, 'I guess you know who's the ace on this team now.'

"I wasn't so cocky a few weeks later," Satchel said with a sigh. "That's when I found myself sent to the reform school."

"The reform school?" Marty said. "I've never seen a reform school. They don't have one here in Indian River."

"Mebbe they don't need one around here," Satchel said, reaching for another helping of potatoes. "Say, this is some grand meal, Mrs. Mitchell."

Amy Mitchell beamed. "Thank you, Mr. Paige—I mean Satchel. And please call me Amy."

"Yes, ma'am."

Satchel sighed. "Yep. You boys don't ever want to be yanked from your fine home and sent to reform school. When they sent me there—for playing hooky and shoplifting—I was real scared. I cried for my mommy for a week.

"After a few days I found out there were things to do at reform school that interested me. I took some classes that taught me a lot. If you're in a place where a lot of facts is flying around, some of them may land inside your head. They goes in through your ears and your eyes and hopefully your brain is smart enough to hang onto some of them. Then I played the drums and sang in the choir."

"But no baseball?" Marty asked.

"Sure there was baseball. That was the best part. They did have baseball there. I was lucky to get a good coach. When he saw I was as tall as he was and skinny as a shovel, he taught me to kick my foot up high so the batter was looking at the soles of my shoes. Like I showed you today, Max. And he taught me to whirl my arm around until it looked like I was releasing the ball right in the batter's face. I scared a lot of them hitters back then."

"You sure enough did, Satch," Josh said quietly. "And you're still scarin' 'em."

Josh pushed his chair back and put his big hand on Marty's shoulder. "Come on outside, son. It'll soon be dark. See if we can't make a catcher out of you."

Marty jumped up. "Sure, Josh, I'll get my mitt. But first, you want to hear a baseball joke?"

Josh said, "Sure. Even though I may have heard it before."

"There was this game played between the Lord's team and the Devil's. The Lord said, 'My team should win. I've got all the great players from the past on my side.'

"And the Devil said, 'Not so fast. I've got all the umpires.'"

Josh and Satch laughed politely, even though they'd heard the joke before.

Josh came right back with a query. "Marty, did you hear about the ballplayer who went blind but he refused to give up the game?"

"No." said Marty. "Come on. How can a blind man stay in baseball."

"Easy," laughed Josh. "He became an umpire."

He pushed Marty gently toward the door.

"Come on. Let's go."

"It seems a shame you'll never get a chance to play in the majors," Harry Mitchell said when Marty and Josh were gone. "And Josh, too. All that talent and only a few fans ever get to see it."

"Don't speak too quick, Mr. Mitchell," Satchel said. "I ain't given up all hope yet. I know I'm gettin' on in years but if I ever get the chance—even if I'm 50 or 60—I'll be sure to make the most of it. I tell myself, Satch, don't look back. Somethin' might be gaining on you."

"How old are you?" said Max, "If you don't mind me asking."

Satchel laughed, white teeth gleaming. "Max, age is a question of mind over matter. If you don't mind, it doesn't matter." He chuckled softly and went on. "People's been asking me my age for as long as I can remember. I don't rightly know. Don't have a birth certificate. I know I'm not too old to pitch another 20 years or so. And I've already pitched for a dozen years or more. Maybe I'll pitch forever."

"Do you think the major leagues will open their doors to coloured players someday?" Max said.

"Hard to say, Max. I figure when the majors are ready for me, I'll be ready for them. I'll probably wind up as the oldest player in major league history."

Big Fella heaved himself out from under the table and wandered into the living room. He growled and then barked twice at a shadow he saw through the front window.

Max jumped up. "Big Fella hears something," he said. "Must be somebody outside. I'll go look."

Max stepped out on the front porch. He noticed a car parked down the street, almost hidden in the lengthening shadows. But he saw no movement.

"Must be somebody visiting the neighbours," he announced when he returned to the kitchen. Big Fella flopped at the feet of Satch.

"Must be a stray cat out there," Satchel said, "or a skunk maybe." He bent down and rubbed Big Fella's head.

"What kind of dog is this?" he asked. "I never saw a dog with so much fur."

"He's a Siberian husky," Max explained. "He won a big sled dog race in Storm Valley last winter."

"Be a shame to have a dog like this in Mobile," he mused. "You'd have to shave him every day just to keep him cool."

Big Fella rolled on his back and Satchel rubbed his belly. Big Fella farted gently. Satch burst out laughing.

"Now look at that," Satch said. "Dogs are wonderful animals. Not an ounce of prejudice in any of 'em. You ever see a white dog look at a black dog with kinky hair and say, 'Don't come near me, boy! You hear! And don't come playin' in my yard.' Most often they'll sniff at each other, just being curious. Then they'll run off and go play together."

Amy Mitchell looked at the clock. "My goodness, it's getting late. And the boys have another game tomorrow. Max, you call Marty and Josh. They're sitting on the back porch talking. I'll show Satchel the guest room."

Satchel said hesitantly, "After you show us the room, do you mind if me and Josh go out for awhile, Mrs. Mitchell. We're in the habit of jogging a mile or two—you know, to stay in shape for baseball—and we've missed our exercise the past day or two. We won't be gone long—maybe an hour or so."

"Of course I don't mind," said Mrs. Mitchell. "The doors are always open here. And I'll leave a light on in your room. And in the bathroom. I've left fresh towels out. You'll want to wash up when you get back. We'll probably be asleep by then."

Harry Mitchell asked, "Shall I leave the porch light on for you fellows?"

"No need," said Josh. "We'll just change into our running shoes and be on our way." A few minutes later, they left by the side door and jogged off into the night.

Harry went to the front door and switched off the light that flooded the front yard. Then he switched it on again. Something on the front lawn had caught his eye. A white sign of some kind. A piece of cardboard? He opened the door and stood on the porch. Then he gasped.

Somebody had planted a crude sign on his lawn. Two male figures somewhat resembling ballplayers were outlined in black paint. Below the figures someone had scrawled the words: DARKIES GO HOME!!

CHAPTER 4

AT THE BALLPARK

On Saturday, Max and Marty were still in a state of shock when they reached the ballpark for the second game in the weekend tournament. Some of their teammates were already there.

"Who could have done such a thing?" Marty asked.

"I'm glad Dad ripped the sign down before Satchel or Josh got back," Max answered. "But they may have seen the sign when they left on their run."

"It's hard to believe someone here in Indian River can be so prejudiced," Marty said.

"Oh, I think there's a lot of prejudice here," Max said. "But a lot of folks try to hide it. Others deny they have any."

"Just between you and I, prejudice is pretty sick," Marty said.

"Between you and me, Marty," Max corrected. "If you say 'between you and I' it's not proper English."

"Thanks, Max," Marty said. "I'm so lucky to have a genius for a brother—just between you and me."

The boys began tossing a baseball back and forth.

They stopped when they heard the sounds of a galloping horse. They turned to see a horse and rider burst through the trees bordering the park.

"It's Sammy Fox," Marty exclaimed, "our star outfielder."

Sammy Fox—or Sammy Running Fox, his given tribal name—lived on the Tumbling Waters Indian reserve a few miles from town. Last winter, Max had recruited Sammy to play hockey for the junior team in town and he had proven himself to be an outstanding player. When Sammy couldn't get a ride into town for games, he rode in on horseback. Now he was doing the same thing during baseball season. The olive-skinned youth dismounted and tied Annabelle in the shade of a nearby tree.

"Hi, fellows," Sammy called out. "I bet you were worried I wouldn't show up today."

"Not at all," Max said, greeting his old friend with a handshake. "We know you always show up."

"Yep," added Marty. "And we expect a few RBIs from you today. We've got to beat Storm Valley to make it to the championship game on Saturday."

"And Dad has two assistants to help him coach us," Marty said excitedly, "Josh Gibson and Satchel Paige. They're the two best ballplayers ever to come to Indian River. Max and I read all about them in last month's *Sporting News*."

A car drove into view and skirted the diamond. "That's Dad's car," said Marty. "He's got Josh and Satchel with him. They volunteered to help us out today, Sammy."

"Wow!" said Sammy. "I could use a few batting tips."

Harry Mitchell parked his car not far from Annabelle.

"Dad's got the rest of the equipment," Max said. "Come on, Sammy, I want you to meet Josh and Satch. They stayed with us last night. This morning Dad took them on a tour of the newspaper office."

The boys helped their father empty the trunk of the car. Balls and bats and bases came tumbling out of a bag, along with resin bags for the pitchers, water bottles, scorecards and a couple of extra well-worn gloves.

"This is our friend Sammy Fox," Max said to Josh and Satchel. "Sammy's from the Indian reserve not far from here. He's our first baseman."

"Well now, we have something in common, Sammy," Satchel Paige said, after greeting Sammy warmly.

"We do?" Sammy said. "You're a first baseman like me?"

"No, it's not that," Satchel said. "I'll show you what I mean. Put your arm next to mine, Sammy. See that. We're both dark-skinned. Only your skin's a shade lighter than mine. Sometimes that can make a world of difference in how a man is treated in this world. If you're a Negro or a native Indian, that is. Or haven't you noticed?"

"Oh, I've noticed, all right," Sammy said with a laugh.

"My skin's too pale," Marty said matter-of-factly. "I get sunburn and freckles."

"I'll bet it's really sensitive, too," Sammy said, winking at Max.

"Is not," snorted Marty. "Why do you say that?"

"Let me show you," said Sammy, grasping Marty by the arm. He pinched Marty hard, close to his elbow.

"Ouch!" Marty cried, jumping back. "That hurt." He began rubbing his arm.

Max laughed and said, "Looks like he proved his point, brother."

"People call me a redskin," Sammy said, turning to Satch and Josh. "Sometimes they even call me a 'dirty redskin.' And I feel like saying, 'My skin's not red, it's brown. And it's not dirty. I wash every day.' "

"Satch and I have to put up with the same thing," Josh said.

"Mostly a lot worse," grunted Satchel.

"Guess I'm pretty lucky," Sammy said. "I'm accepted now because I play on the junior hockey and baseball teams. Otherwise…"

"Sammy's a star on our teams," Max said.

"That's great," Josh said. "At least you can play with whites. We show up on a ball field with white players and we'd be chased out of town."

"Maybe we'd be lynched," said Josh.

"I live with my people on a reserve," Sammy ventured. "It's not like we're living in town."

"I get it," Satch said. "They put you far enough away for it not to be a problem. Boys, what do you think the reaction in town would be if a Negro family moved in?"

Max said, "Gee, I honestly don't know. I hope there'd be no problems. There've never been any Negro families in town."

"I think most people in town are like my folks," Marty said. "They're not prejudiced."

"Your folks are special," Satchel said. "Josh and I were surprised when they took us in. But I'll bet you a bundle of folks don't feel like they do."

Max thought of the sign thrown on the front lawn of the Mitchell residence and frowned. Maybe Satch was right.

Sammy said to Satch, "It's such an honour to meet you and Josh. I'll bet you've been telling Max and Marty some interesting stories."

"I was telling them how we kicked around the Negro leagues for a number of years," Satch said. "Not to brag, but I began winning so many games I lost track of the number. In 1926 I had a 25-game win streak and was winning number 26 easy when my infielders gave up three straight errors in the ninth inning. I was so hot with them I did a crazy thing. The bases were loaded with two out. I called my outfielders into the mound and told them to sit down on the grass. 'I don't need no outfielders for this last batter,' I told them. The crowd went wild when I threw my bee ball for three quick strikes. Game over. We win."

"Your bee ball?" Max asked.

"Yep. I had my bee ball—my fastball—and my hesitation pitch and lots of other pitches. There was my two-hump blooper and my barber ball— guaranteed to give a batter a close shave whether he wanted one or not. And my arm was durable. I once pitched 165 days in a row when we was barnstorming around the country. I had to pitch every game. If I didn't, the folks wouldn't come out to see the game. But there I go, talking about myself again."

Just then Harry Mitchell strode toward them after handing his starting lineup to the umpire. "You boys going to play ball or are you going to talk to Satch and Josh all afternoon?" he asked. "Max, you'll be playing third base today. Darrel Dugan will be pitching. Satchel may pitch two days in a row, or even four or five, but I'm saving your arm for Saturday's big game."

Darrel Dugan was warming up on the sidelines when Satchel approached him.

"Harry Mitchell asked me to help out today. I'm a pitcher like you," Satchel said.

"So?" Darrel grunted as he continued to throw his warmup pitches.

Satchel instantly felt the same hint of animosity from Darrel that he'd felt from his father, Sheriff Dugan, following the incident with Mrs. Anderson. He said, backing off, "Well, I'm around if you need me. I'm here to give advice…"

"Don't need advice," Darrel mumbled, turning his back on Satchel and rubbing up the ball. "If I do need some, I'll ask. You got it, coach?" Darrel emphasized the word coach—making it sound almost like a dirty word.

"Sure. I got it, kid," Satchel said, walking away. "Have a good game."

But Darrel Dugan didn't have a good game. The lefty walked the first three batters he faced. All three tested Marty Mitchell's arm by attempting to steal second base. And all three were thrown out to end the inning.

"Wow!" exclaimed Max, slapping his brother on the back when they came to the bench. "You've never thrown bullets to second like that before. What's got into you? All three of those runners thought they could beat your throw."

"They could have maybe—if it was yesterday," Marty said. "But last night Josh taught me how to release the ball faster. And how to get my body behind it. And where to aim the ball to save a split second. It worked! He's a great teacher."

"Good work, Marty," Josh said. "I'm proud of you."

Max had noticed something the three runners had done before Marty had smartly tossed them out at second. All had taken big leads on Darrel Dugan. He talked it over with Satchel.

"Maybe you could tell Darrel how to hold the runners on first," he suggested. "If he lets them lead off like that, Marty won't be able to throw them out like he did in the first inning."

Satchel said, "You're right, Max. But Darrel made it clear he doesn't want my advice. So it's up to your father to tell him. He's the manager."

"No, he won't listen to Dad either," Max remarked. "Or any of his teammates. The only person he'll listen to is his father."

"Too bad," said Satchel. "The kid has a good fastball. But he relies on it too much. If he mixed in more curveballs, he'd keep opposing batters off balance. But again, I'm not going to tell him that unless he asks."

"He won't ask," Max said. "His Dad told him major league scouts look for fastball pitchers. The harder you throw the more chance you'll make it in pro ball. His dad told him to lay off the curveballs."

"Seems to me he's getting poor advice," Satchel sighed. "When I was his age I already had three or four different pitches down pat."

The game reached the seventh inning with the score tied 4–4. Max proved to be as steady at third base as he was on the mound. He made three run-saving plays at third base and had chased down a high foul ball, catching it just as it was about to fall into the seats along the third base line. The hometown fans gave him a loud ovation after each play.

By the top of the eighth inning, the Chatsworth batters began feasting on Darrel Dugan's fastballs. Marty, his catcher, signalled several times for a curve and a changeup but Darrel shook his head. The opposing batters soon caught on. They realized Darrel wasn't throwing anything but speed—and batted balls soon flew in all directions. Sammy Fox made an outstanding catch, leaping high in the air to snag a ball headed for the outfield. Terry Buchanan, the Millers' centre fielder, raced back and caught a hard hit ball over his shoulder. Two balls were hit sharply through the infield for base hits but the runners stayed close to their bases, fearful of Marty's throwing arm. With two out, Marty came through with a sparkling catch of a foul ball to end the inning.

Reynolds, the Chatsworth pitcher, tired in the bottom of the eighth. Marty singled to lead off and took second on Buchanan's sacrifice bunt. Sammy Fox drew a walk. Max singled off the third baseman's glove and Marty scooted into third base. The Chatsworth manager jogged to the mound and took the ball from Reynolds. A relief pitcher, a tall kid named O'Reilly, came in and struck out Darrel Dugan on three pitches and McBean, a pinch hitter, on four. The score remained tied at 4–4.

Top of the ninth.

Dugan trudged slowly to the mound. He was tired. But the Millers had no relief pitchers. On the sidelines, Satchel Paige was caught up in the drama as the game neared its finish. He clapped his hands together and shouted encouragement, trying to energize his team's pitcher from the sidelines. "Come on, Dugie, you can do it. Only three more outs, boy."

There was a roar of objection from the stands. Sheriff Dugan rushed toward Satchel, shouting. "Don't ever call my son, 'boy.'" He pointed a large finger at Satchel's chest. "You're the 'boy' here, not Darrel. And don't you forget it."

Satchel was shocked. He hadn't intended to insult anyone. He was only trying to help. All chatter on the field and in the stands stopped. Everyone was stunned by the lawman's outburst.

Sheriff Dugan turned away for a moment and then turned back again.

"And don't be telling my son how to pitch. You and your bee ball and your hesitation pitch! My son throws heat, man. Major league stuff. He's faster than you ever were, old man. Stay away from him!"

Sheriff Dugan then did something extraordinary. He looked out to the mound and shouted at Darrel, "Come on with me, son. You're through for the day."

"But Dad," Darrel protested, "I'm only three outs away..."

"Come off that mound this instant!" Sheriff Dugan screamed in fury.

Slowly, Darrel obeyed. He kicked at the resin bag and shuffled off the field. His head sagged and his cheeks blushed crimson. His father threw an arm around his shoulders and led him away to the police car parked nearby, its engine idling. They drove off, dust from the spinning wheels drifting across the diamond.

There was a buzz of conversation in the stands.

"Why'd he do that?" asked a fan. "The kid was pitching great ball."

"Dugie was real ticked off," said another. "He can be real mean when he wants to be."

Top of the ninth and there was no pitcher on the mound for the Millers.

Harry Mitchell signalled for a timeout and the umpire granted it. Harry called his team together in the middle of the diamond.

"Any of you fellows know how to pitch?" he quipped, breaking the tension with a smile. He appeared ready to toss the baseball to the first one who answered.

"Max is our only other pitcher but we're saving him for Sunday," said Terry Buchanan.

"How about you pitching, Marty?" asked Sammy Fox. "You showed a great arm so far today."

Marty grinned. "I'd do it but I can't pitch and catch too. I'm good but I'm not that good."

"You've got that right, brother," Max said, taking the ball from his father's hand. "Dad, it's only one inning. I'll finish up and still be fresh for Sunday's game."

"Attaboy, Max," Satchel said. "Oops! Sorry. I used that word 'boy' again."

Everybody laughed and the umpire, standing nearby, chuckled too. Then he shouted, "Play ball!"

The Chatsworth batters groaned when they saw Max take the mound. They'd rather have faced somebody else—anybody else. They groaned even louder when Max struck out two of their best hitters and got the third man to ground out to first.

But they were relieved when Indian River failed to score in the bottom of the ninth. The tenth inning came and went. So did the 11th and 12th. Still no winning run. Both teams came close but neither could bring a runner home from third base.

Max began to tire. He'd thrown a lot of baseballs in the past two days and he hadn't expected the game to go extra innings. He bore down in the top of the 13th and struck out all three Chatsworth batters.

When he came up to bat in the bottom of the inning, there were two outs and runners on first and second—there on walks.

The tall kid O'Reilly glared in at Max. He wanted to walk Max but he didn't dare. He didn't intend to load the bases with Sammy Fox coming up next.

"Hit this, Mitchell," he grunted, as he lurched into his windup and hurled his fastball at the plate. The ball was two inches off the corner of the plate but Max reached out and smacked it. Pow! The ball soared into deep right field and settled in a grove of pine trees far beyond the outfield fence. Home run!

The Indian River bench erupted and players rushed out to greet Max as he skipped around the bases and crossed home plate. They hoisted him off his feet and pounded him on the back. Somewhere along the way he lost his cap. But he never lost his smile.

CHAPTER 5

THE UNDESIRABLES

"Let's go to Merry Mabel's to celebrate," Marty said to Max. "I'll treat you to an ice cream sundae for hitting that homer. It's the longest one you ever hit."

"Okay by me," said Max. "Come on, Josh and Satch. And you too, Mom and Dad."

"Be with you in a minute," Satch said. He and Josh were helping collect bats and balls.

Max noted the look of concern on Marty's face. He laughed. "Don't worry, Marty. You won't have to pay for six. I'll go halfers with you, okay? It's the least we can do for Josh and Satch after the great tips they gave us."

"You fellows go on ahead," their father said. "Your mother and I have to go to the *Review* to finish up some newspaper business. We'll see you at Merry Mabel's later."

"I'll walk my bike," suggested Marty. "I suppose yours is a goner."

"That's right. A kid I know dragged it home. He said he could use the seat and the bell." Max sighed. "Guess I'll have to save up for a new one."

"Satch offered you some money for one."

"I know. But I can't take it. It wasn't his fault the bus lost its brakes. And he'll need money for legal costs."

Marty shrugged. "Anyway, we can show Josh and Satch all the great tourist attractions in Indian River."

"Sure," Max said. "But after the town hall there's not much else to see."

"And Satch has already seen the jail," Marty quipped.

They arrived at the restaurant and entered. Merry Mabel was at the cash register and looked up in surprise when she saw the Mitchell brothers accompanied by two dark-skinned strangers.

"Hi, Mabel," Max greeted her warmly. "We won the ball game. Now it's time for ice cream."

Mabel appeared flustered. "That's good news, boys," she said. But she didn't sound enthusiastic.

Marty started for a table up front, near the big picture window overlooking the street. "Good. Our favourite table is open," he said.

"Wait a minute, Marty," Mabel said, reaching for some menus. "Uh, sorry, boys. That table's reserved. I've got a party coming in a few minutes. But I can put you in the back."

"Reserved?" Marty asked. "I never knew you took reservations."

"I said I can put you in the back," Mabel said testily. She tried hard not to look at the two strangers. "Take it or leave it."

It dawned on Max that Mabel was upset. And it was all because Satch and Josh were in her restaurant. She wanted to hide them at a table in the back. If they sat at the big table up front, people passing by would see them through the window. Max was appalled. This was Mabel, a woman everyone loved and respected.

The tension was broken when Trudy Reeves, a high school friend of the Mitchell brothers, left a booth along the side wall and rushed forward. Trudy was a skilled hockey player and horse-woman, good enough at hockey to play with and against men and so adept as a harness-race driver to have won the famous Hambletonian. Someone had even written a book about her feat called *Wizard the Wonder Horse.*

"Max! Marty!" she greeted them. "We've been waiting for you. We're so glad you brought Mr. Paige and Mr. Gibson. Come sit with us in our booth. There's plenty of room. We can talk about the game today."

Trudy took Josh and Satchel by the arm and led them to the booth. Her girlfriend Sandy Hope was there, smiling broadly through the braces on her teeth.

"What an honour to meet you," Sandy said to Satch and Josh. "I follow baseball avidly. I even brought my autograph book and a baseball. I hope you'll sign them for me."

"It would be our pleasure," Satchel said. He shook his head sadly. "If only we had learned how to write."

Sandy's hand shot to her mouth. "Oh, I'm sorry," she wailed. "I never dreamed..."

Josh burst out laughing. "Satch is kidding you, little lady. He can write and read with the best of them. And I'm no slouch, either."

They signed Sandy's book and baseball and she thanked them profusely. She reached into a bag and held up another autographed baseball.

"This one was signed by the great Babe Ruth," she said proudly. "My dad got it for me. He went to training camp with the Yankees a few years ago and roomed with Babe Ruth. He says this ball will be worth a fortune some day."

Satchel examined the ball. "That's Babe Ruth's signature all right. He signed a ball for me once, in Chicago. And your dad's right. Fans are beginning to pay big money for souvenirs like this."

"Yep," added Josh. "Someday you might even get a few pennies for the ball we just signed."

Sandy laughed. "I'm never going to sell these baseballs—yours or Babe Ruth's. One is signed by the game's greatest slugger, the other by the world's best pitcher. They mean a lot to me."

"Did you know they just opened a new Hall of Fame for baseball players?" Josh asked. "It's in Cooperstown, New York, and Babe Ruth was one of the first players inducted."

"That's great news," Sandy said.

"You don't play the game, do you, Sandy?" Satch asked.

"I wish," answered Sandy. "My dad wanted a boy and got me—a skinny little girl with freckles. And now I have these metal braces in my mouth. Ugly braces."

Satch hushed her. "Remember the ugly duckling turned into a beautiful swan," he said. "I thought I was an ugly duckling as a child. Then my mother read me that story about the swan. I felt better after that. And look at me today." He flashed his white teeth. "I'm such a handsome devil."

Josh groaned and made a face.

"Look again!" he said, laughing loudly. "You're still an ugly duckling."

"Less noise over there," Mabel shouted across the room. The teenagers were surprised.

"Mabel's got a bee in her bonnet today," Trudy said. "I wonder why."

"You were telling us about your interest in base-ball," Satch prompted Sandy, speaking almost in a whisper.

"I was, wasn't I?" Sandy answered. "My dad taught me to hit and to field ground balls. I play sandlot ball with the boys in the neighbourhood."

"You should see her field those grounders," Trudy said. "Sandy's great. And she hits better than most of the boys. Not as well as Max and Marty, of course. But almost in their class."

The ice cream arrived. Sandy was in her element. Baseball was in her blood. She wanted to know all about the careers of Satch and Josh. "When did you first start playing organized ball, Mr. Paige?" she asked.

"It was 1924—about 12 years ago," said Satchel, counting on his fingers. "I went right to a ballpark in Mobile and asked the manager there for a tryout. He laughed and said, 'Go home, kid.'

"I said, 'It's your loss, mister. I can throw faster than all those shufflers you got on your roster. Why, I can nip the frosting off a cake with my fastball. I can put it over a gum wrapper at home plate nine times out of ten.'

"Sure I was braggin' but mebbe the way I said those things got his attention. He didn't say much.

46

Just threw me a ball. Then he picked up a bat and stood in at the plate. 'Prove it, kid,' he said.

"I took a few warm-up tosses and those pitches sounded like rifle shots when they hit the catcher's mitt. I grinned and asked, 'You ready, mister?'

"He nodded and I threw 12 pitches past him, each one cracking into that glove. He fanned on all 12. That man threw his arms up and walked to the mound. 'You're sure a marvel, kid. I didn't even see that last one. Do you pitch that fast consistently?'

"'Well, I pitch that way all the time if that's what you mean.'

"He laughed out loud and said, 'That's what I mean—consistently.'"

Satchel leaned back in the booth and grinned at Sandy.

"Young lady, I learned me a new word that day."

Josh said, "Satch is fast, all right. Why, he can turn out the light and jump into bed before the room gets dark."

The booth filled with laughter.

"Hush," said Max, putting a finger to his lips. "Mabel's glaring at us."

"So you had major league ability when you were real young—still a teenager?" Sandy all but whispered. "But you were shunned by all the best teams, right?"

"I learned in a hurry that the best clubs in organized ball were all white teams. No Negroes allowed. One manager told me, 'Satchel, if I could paint you white and the paint would stick, I'd sign you in a minute.'

"Another manager actually wanted to paint me. Said he'd pay me 500 dollars if I'd do it. He had a bucket of paint ready and a brush. Told me the paint would wash off in the shower after the game. I said, 'You crazy, man? You ever hear of the word dignity? I'd love to play in a white man's league but not that badly.' I still had some pride, see."

"I was right there when it happened," Josh added. He smiled broadly. "That's when I accidentally nudged the bucket with my foot and the white paint spilled all over the man's new shoes."

Marty snickered.

Satchel said, "I guess I knew right then that all roads to the major leagues were closed to me— and anyone my colour—probably forever."

Josh shook his head sadly. "Even though Satch wins 50 or 60 games a year and averages 15 strikeouts a game. Nobody's ever done that."

"Now you young folks are the only people in town who even knows about our baseball careers," Satchel said. "This is all very flattering."

"I know about all the ballplayers," Sandy said proudly. "Did you ever hear the name Monte Ward, Mr. Paige?"

"Can't say that I have."

"Monte Ward was only 18 years old when he pitched for the Providence club. He won 22 games his first season and 47 the next. You could look it up, if you don't believe me."

"Oh, I believe you, miss. How come I never pitched against him?"

Sandy laughed. "That's because he pitched back in 1878. Three years later he blew out his arm and became an infielder. Played for 17 seasons."

Satch was amazed at Sandy's knowledge of baseball. "You must have been born in a dugout," he observed with a chuckle.

Josh joined in the conversation. "Here's a name for you, miss. Iron Man McGinnity. Bet you don't know about him."

"Indeed I do, Mr. Gibson. McGinnity once won five games in six days when he was with the Dodgers and ten games in 12 days when he was with the Giants. That was back at the turn of the century."

"You're amazing," Josh said. "And McGinnity pitched both ends of a doubleheader five times in his career."

"My turn to try and stump her," Satch said. "Okay, tell me where Babe Ruth hit his first home run."

"Oh, that's easy," Sandy said. "It was in one of the few games he played in the minors. In Toronto in 1914. At Hanlan's Point on Toronto Island. Now tell me this. What position did he play that day?"

"Outfield, of course," Satch replied instantly.

"Nope. He pitched a one-hit shutout over the Toronto Maple Leafs. And one newspaper claimed the home run he hit went clear across Lake Ontario and landed in Buffalo, New York."

"That part I don't believe," Satchel said. "But I must say you know more about baseball than anyone I ever met."

"You're a regular encyclopedia of the game," Josh confirmed.

"Thank you," Sandy said, flashing her braces. "My whole family plans on coming to the game when you play here in Indian River in a few days. Dad says you and Josh are about the two best players in the game today and that includes all the major leaguers. It's so sad they won't let you play with the best teams around."

"Someday they'll let us in," Josh predicted. "We just have to be patient. It may come too late for us but our kids and grandkids will get a chance, maybe."

"It must be awful to be discriminated against," Sandy said.

"Heck, we're nervous just sitting here," Josh said, looking around. "In some places down south, we'd be hauled out the door and beaten up. You can bet Mabel's going to breathe easier when we leave."

"But you're almost in the same boat as us, little lady," Josh said, smiling.

"What do you mean?"

"I mean they won't let you play ball for the Millers, will they? Why? Because you're a girl. That's a kind of discrimination, too."

"But I'm not good enough to play for the local team," Sandy protested.

"How do you know?" Josh asked. "Did you ever try out? Did you ever ask Mr. Mitchell to give you a chance?"

"No. I always thought..."

"You thought the game was only for boys," Josh said. "Let me tell you about a pitcher named Jackie Mitchell. She was a 17-year-old pitcher who struck out Babe Ruth and Lou Gehrig, two great Yankee stars, in an exhibition game a few years ago. So don't give up your baseball dreams."

"Tell you what, Sandy," added Satchel. "You can be our bat girl when we come back in a few days to play in Indian River."

Sandy bounced up and down in the booth. "That would be wonderful," she said. "I can't wait."

"But what about your tour?" Trudy asked. "Did you have to cancel some games because your bus broke down?"

"We postponed three of them," Satchel explained. "Bus should be ready to go in a few days. We'll play a couple of games in towns north of here and come back here to Indian River for a big game a week from Saturday. Once I settle a small legal problem, that is."

"And who will you play here—an all-star team?"

"Doesn't matter who we play. We beat 'em all," Satch said confidently. "It sounds like bragging but it's the truth. We hardly ever lose."

Marty spoke up. "They'll be playing us—the Millers. And we're going to beat the pants off them. Max is going to shut them out with his pitching and I'll hit about four home runs off Satchel. They'll wish they'd never heard of Indian River before we're through."

The burst of laughter that greeted Marty's prediction echoed throughout Merry Mabel's.

But the owner, standing by the cash register, didn't laugh. A frown was frozen on Mabel's face and she glanced over at their table frequently. It was as though she was hoping the Mitchell brothers and their strange friends would soon leave her establishment. Meanwhile, the big table by the window remained empty.

"We'll see about that boast," Satchel said. "You boys are good but not good enough to whip old Satch. And I'm not going to just let you win, just because your mommy and daddy was nice to us."

Later, outside the restaurant, after Trudy and Sandy had left for home, the Mitchell brothers and the two ballplayers waited for Harry and Amy Mitchell to come back from the newspaper office to pick them up.

Next door to Merry Mabel's was Dapper Dan's Barber Shop. Dapper Dan had just finished cutting a customer's hair and was using a soft brush to whisk loose hairs from the man's back and shoulders. He pocketed a quarter for his efforts and walked his customer to the door. Dapper Dan spotted Max and Marty on the sidewalk and called out, "Max! You need a haircut. You better get in here. Chair's empty. Nobody's waiting." Dapper Dan nodded at Josh and Satchel. "Hi yah, fellows."

Max laughed and said, "No haircut today, Dan. Trudy likes me with long hair. She's afraid you'll give me one of those brush cuts you're famous for."

"How about you, Marty?" Dan said.

Before Marty could reply, Josh stepped forward. "I could use a haircut, sir, brush cut or not," he said. "Do we have time, Max?"

Max was about to say they did have time, when he heard Dan sputter, "Sorry, pal. I...uh...just remembered. Got a dentist appointment down the street." He looked at his watch. "By golly, I'm late."

He stepped back inside his shop, slammed the door and placed a CLOSED sign in his window.

Josh gave Max and Marty an amused look. "Often it's a dentist appointment. Or a funeral they forgot. Or they've got to run down to the bank before it closes."

"Sometimes that CLOSED sign goes up when we're still a block away," chuckled Satchel. "You try to get used to it. That barber was quick, wasn't he? Poor old Merry Mabel didn't know what to do with us."

Satchel reached out and tapped Marty on the shoulder. "What were you saying earlier, son. Something about most people in this town not being prejudiced. Well, most say they're not prejudiced. Some will swear they're not. Well, I believe we just met a couple of folks who aren't sure about their feelings—whether they want to admit it or not."

"I'm really surprised," said Max. "I would never have thought Merry Mabel or Dapper Dan would act that way." He found himself wondering if one of them had placed the sign on the front lawn.

"Me, neither," said Marty. "People making such a big deal out of skin colour. It's bull! Aren't we all pretty much the same underneath that skin? Underneath aren't we all red meat and red blood and pink muscles and white bones and purple arteries and blue veins. If they opened any one of us up, isn't that what they'd find?"

"Pretty much," Josh agreed. "Lots of colours inside all of us."

"Even some browns and yellows," Marty said, bursting into laughter. "If you know what I mean. Like when you go to the bath…"

"Yeah, we know," Max interrupted. "Don't be gross. And you forgot brains, Marty. Brains are white, I think. But if they opened you up, they might be hard pressed to find one. And if they did, they'd probably think a golf ball had found its way in there somehow."

"Huh!" snorted Marty. "And if they opened you up they'd say, 'Look! It's Max Mitchell's brain, all right. It's as small as an aspirin and it looks brand new. Never been used.' "

Max laughed and playfully threw one arm around Marty's neck and squeezed hard. "Say 'Uncle,'" he demanded.

But Josh intervened and pulled the brothers apart. "You boys stop horsing around," he admonished them. "Merry Mabel's watching out the window. Next thing you know she'll be calling the sheriff. He'll arrest me for common assault—just for trying to keep you two apart."

"If we stand here much longer, he can charge us with loitering," added Satch grimly. "It's happened to us before."

Just then, Harry and Amy Mitchell drove up in the family car.

"Josh and Satch, get in quick!" Mr. Mitchell urged. "You too, Max. Something's happened. Something serious. Marty, ride home on your bike. We'll tell you all about it when you get there."

CHAPTER 6

MRS. ANDERSON GOES MISSING

"What is it, Dad? What's happened?" Marty asked, when they were home and seated around the kitchen table.

"The sheriff called my office with some shocking news," he replied. "It's Mrs. Anderson. She's disappeared and her home has been robbed."

"Oh oh," murmured Satchel. "You know what that means, Josh."

"Sure do," said Josh with a sigh. "It means that old sheriff will be coming around asking questions. He'll be thinking we had somethin' to do with it. You watch."

"But why?" Marty said. "Don't be silly. You two haven't done anything wrong."

"That's true," said Satch. "But you can wager someone will be wondering if we did."

"There's no reason for anyone to suspect you and Josh," Max said. "You've been with us every minute since you got here. We'll swear to it."

Josh and Satch exchanged uneasy glances.

"I'm going to drive over to Mrs. Anderson's," Mr. Mitchell said. "She's a widow and she has no family. I hope she's just wandered off. And that nothing...well, nothing more serious has happened to her."

"We hope so, too," Satch said. "She did hit her head when she fell the other day."

"But she went to the hospital," Marty said. "They checked her out and released her."

"Whoever robbed her wouldn't have known that," Mr. Mitchell said. "They probably thought her house was empty. I'm going over there to get the full story. Everyone sit tight at home until I get back."

Sheriff Dugan, his son Darrel and a deputy— Billy Calhoon—were at the Anderson home when Mr. Mitchell arrived. Carrying his camera and a notebook he got out of his car and scrutinized the old home. It was set back from the road, situated on an isolated lane on the far side of town. He took a couple of photographs of the dilapidated house, noting it was sadly lacking in paint.

"No sign of her yet," Sheriff Dugan reported. "But her house is a mess. Somebody trashed it. Hard to say what's missing. Some jewellery, some cash, I'll bet. Mrs. Anderson wasn't a big believer in banks."

"We talked to all of her neighbours," Billy Calhoon said. "Nobody heard or saw anything. But then, they're all a good distance away. A nurse from the hospital came by an hour ago to check on her condition. Found the house ransacked. Nurse called us right away."

"There are no lights on in the house," Harry Mitchell said.

Sheriff Dugan shook his head. "Mrs. Anderson is known to be cheap. No, let me call it frugal. To save on electricity she lives by candlelight a lot of the time. Has a wood-burning stove in the kitchen for cooking and heat. But somebody knew she had cash in the house."

"Could Mrs. Anderson have driven somewhere—to a relative's house, maybe?" Harry Mitchell asked.

"Nope. She doesn't own a car," the sheriff replied. "She's got to be close by—unless she was kidnapped." He turned and looked Harry Mitchell straight in the eye. "Where are those two friends of yours, the Negro ballplayers?" he asked.

"They're in my home. Why do you ask?"

"Oh, nothin'," murmured the sheriff. "Just wonderin'."

"We'd better get a search party organized," said Billy Calhoon.

"You'd better bring those darkies over here," the sheriff said to Harry Mitchell. "I want to talk with them. And bring Max and Marty, too. We can fan out and search the immediate area. If we don't find her, we'll have to bring in more folks to help out."

"I can do that," Harry Mitchell said. He patted his camera. "Got some photos of the house," he said. "This story will be in the *Review* this week."

The search party of seven men and a woman—including Satch and Josh and Amy Mitchell who insisted on coming along—fanned out in all directions leading from the Anderson house. The searchers walked through the tall grass and the thick underbrush. They slogged through a muddy gully and worked their way through a nearby woods.

It was Max who first discovered a clue to Mrs. Anderson's disappearance.

"Marty, come here!" he shouted. "Look at this!"

Marty rushed to join his brother and saw him pointing at some crushed grass on the slope of a hill.

"Looks like something—an animal, maybe, or perhaps a human—was through here and knocked the grass down."

"You're right, Max. It could have been Mrs. Anderson," Marty said excitedly. "Let's look down the hill."

The boys followed the trail and almost toppled down an embankment, which fell away sharply.

"There she is!" Marty shouted, reaching for Max to hold his balance. "She's fallen down the slope. She's not moving."

"Go back for the sheriff," Max ordered Marty. "We mustn't touch anything. This may be a crime scene."

Moments later, Sheriff Dugan was bending over the body of Mrs. Anderson. He searched for a pulse. Then he put his head close to hers. The other searchers stayed back, waiting anxiously for him to say something.

Then he stood and announced, "The lady is alive. Her pulse is weak and she's unconscious." He ordered his deputy to run to the nearest house and call for an ambulance.

"Nice work," he said to Max and Marty. "She either fell or was thrown into that gully. Her body was hard to spot."

"Thrown?" Marty gasped. "You mean somebody tried to kill her?"

"At first glance, it looks that way," the sheriff replied. "She's badly bruised as if somebody beat her. I suspect whoever robbed her house did this. My guess is she caught them in the act and they tried to do away with her."

"Sheriff, you just said 'they,'" Max said. "Why do you think it was two people who did this?"

Sheriff Dugan looked grim. "Because she mumbled something to me a moment ago. I heard her say 'two darkies' did this to me."

With that he pulled a revolver from the holster on his hip and held it by his side. He turned to face Josh and Satchel.

"Where were you two last night?" he demanded.

"We were at the Mitchell's," Josh said. "You can ask them if it's not true."

"They were," confirmed Harry Mitchell. "I swear it."

"All night?" asked the sheriff.

"Sure, all night, except for...well, never mind."

"Hey, what's that mean?" barked the sheriff.

"Well," Harry stammered, "they went out jogging before we went to bed. But they weren't gone but a few minutes."

"You shouldn't have let them do that, Harry," the sheriff admonished the newspaper publisher. "They were in your custody, remember? That means full supervision."

"I never thought..."

"You should have. Turns out you were saddled with two dangerous criminals," the sheriff said, his revolver drawing nervous glances from Josh and Satch. "What time did they get back?"

Harry sighed and said, "Honestly, I don't know. I fell asleep." He turned to Amy and the boys. "Do any of you know when Josh and Satch came back?"

Amy shook her head.

Max said, "Gee, Dad, I don't know. But it couldn't have been long." He desperately wanted to say he'd heard his friends come in. But he couldn't outright lie about it.

"How about it, boys?" The sheriff asked, turning to Satch and Josh. "What time did you return to the Mitchell house?"

"Don't know," Satchel answered. "I don't own a watch. Don't like to see time slippin' away."

Josh shrugged. "Sometime before midnight," he said.

In the distance they heard the siren of the ambulance.

"If Mrs. Anderson dies, you fellows are the most likely suspects," he said to Josh and Satchel. "The only suspects, in my opinion." He turned to Harry Mitchell who was taking notes. This would be front page news in the next issue of the *Review*. "Your house guests had lots of time to do it," the sheriff said. "The first time I spotted them," he smirked, "I knew they were going to be trouble. But I didn't think I'd be charging them with attempted murder."

"Hey, Billy," he called out. "Put your handcuffs on that one." He nodded toward Josh. "And I'll put mine on the famous baseball pitcher." He leaned in close to Satchel as he snapped the cuffs in place and sneered in his ear, "Fella, it's my belief you'll do all your pitching from now on in the penitentiary—on the prison baseball team."

The Mitchells were in a state of shock when they arrived back home.

"I can't believe Josh and Satch would do such a thing," Marty said, almost in tears. "They couldn't have."

"We could look through the guest room," Max suggested. "See if any of Mrs. Anderson's stuff is there."

"No, we won't do that," Mr. Mitchell stated. "If you truly believe they are innocent, there's no need to do that. Well, do you believe in them or not?"

"We believe in them," Max and Marty uttered in unison.

"But if they didn't do it, who did?" Max asked. "We don't have much crime in Indian River. Not many folks are out in the streets late at night. Robbing old widows and beating them up. The sheriff seems to have made up his mind that Josh and Satch robbed Mrs. Anderson."

"It could have been the nurse," Marty suggested.

"Impossible," their mother scoffed. "I've known that nurse for years. She's sweeter than corn syrup."

"If poor Mrs. Anderson dies, Satch and Josh may be charged with murder," Max said soberly. "And we'll have to testify they left our house to go jogging. I wish one of us had heard them come in."

"We can visit Josh and Satch in jail tomorrow," Marty suggested. "Bring them some sandwiches and some books to read. We can try to cheer them up. They'll have to appear in court in a couple of days. And they'll have to cancel some more exhibition games."

"Maybe Dad can help arrange bail for them," Max said. "But even if he does, they won't be allowed to leave town."

"I was shocked when the sheriff said Mrs. Anderson told him 'two darkies' were her attackers," Marty remarked. "That makes the sheriff's case awfully strong."

"I wonder about that, too," Max said. "She was barely conscious when she said it. Groggy and confused. Then she lapsed into a coma. I sure hope she survives. I'd like to hear her tell what she really saw, what really happened."

CHAPTER 7

THE CHAMPIONSHIP GAME

"Play ball!" howled the burly umpire. He took a small broom from his hip pocket and leaned over to dust off home plate. In doing so, he split the seam in the back of his pants and the crowd tittered at the sight of his underwear.

The ump was unfazed. "It's happened before," he called back to the crowd. "Now home plate is as clean as my underwear."

"Let's hope they both stay that way," shouted a female voice. It was Sandy Hope, who was throwing a baseball back and forth with Trudy Reeves on the sidelines.

The crowd laughed.

"Play ball!" was the umpire's response.

On the home team's bench, Harry Mitchell, manager of the Millers, was downcast. He'd turned in his starting line-up to the umpire and he'd been forced to make a change. Sammy Fox, always so reliable, had not shown up on Annabelle. Horse and rider were conspicuously absent.

"I just hope he's all right," Max said to his father. "Sammy never misses a game, winter or summer."

"Well, he's missed this one," said Mr. Mitchell grimly.

The coach felt a tug on his sleeve. He turned to face a teenage girl with a face covered with freckles. "I can play first base, Mr. Mitchell," she said earnestly. "I'll play in Sammy's place."

Harry Mitchell was surprised. Somehow he managed not to laugh out loud.

"I don't think so, miss," he said. "But I appreciate the offer. I've got young Jimmy Jansen as a backup."

"That's okay," the girl said. "But I'll be around if you need me."

Harry Mitchell turned to Max.

"Who was she?" he asked.

"Oh, that's Sandy Hope," Max answered. "She loves baseball. Trudy says she's really good at it."

"I'll keep her in mind—if we're really desperate," his father said. "But I've decided to put young Jansen at first. Even though he's weak on ground balls." He put a hand on his son's shoulder. "Your arm okay? You've had a busy week."

"My arm's fine," Max assured his father. "Let's go!"

It was the championship game of the tournament. The Millers versus the Chatsworth Cougars. And the Millers were missing one of their best hitters and fielders. But Darrel Dugan was back. He'd convinced his dad to let him play. "Why not?" his dad had said. "Satchel Paige won't be there to yell at you."

While Max threw his warm-up tosses in to Marty, his mind was brooding on other matters. *I wish Sammy was here*, he thought. *Without him I'll have to bear down a little harder. And my arm is a wee bit sore.*

Then Marty was in front of him, barking into his face. "Are you daydreaming or what?" his brother demanded. "First batter is waiting at the plate and you seem to be somewhere in space. Are you okay?"

Max blushed. He had been daydreaming. "Yeah, I'm okay. I'm fine," he muttered. "I'm ready. Let's play."

It took him an inning or two to find a groove. He gave up a double to the leadoff man in the second inning, then walked the next batter. The Chatsworth third baseman, batting next, drilled a grounder to first. But Jimmy Jansen failed to field the ball and it sailed through his legs. The runner scored from second and the Cougars took a 1–0 lead. Max retired the side with a double play he started himself and a strikeout, his first of the afternoon.

But Gary "Goose" Goslin, a tall lefthander for the Cougars, was feeding the Millers a number of knuckleballs, a pitch he'd been working on all summer. They swung and missed, swung and missed. Through six innings, Goslin had the Miller batters in his hip pocket. He began thinking of every pitcher's dream—a no-hitter. Maybe even a perfect game.

By then, Max had found his rhythm. He felt strong and his arm was loose. He too began piling up strikeouts. He was determined to battle Goslin to the finish. The Mitchell brothers didn't like Goslin. He was an arrogant youth and his behaviour off the field left something to be desired. He was a bully who'd been in trouble with the law more than once. The Chatsworth police chief had arrested him twice for shoplifting.

"Somehow we'll find a way to hit your knuckleball," Max muttered as he left the mound at the end of the seventh.

As he strode toward the Millers' bench, he saw a commotion along the sidelines. There was Sammy Fox! Sammy had leaped off Annabelle and rushed toward the team bench where his mates greeted him enthusiastically.

"Where you been, Sammy? What happened?" he was asked.

Max noticed that Sammy's face was marked. One eye was black, his lip was cut and there were bruises on his arms.

"What happened, Sammy?" asked Max. "Were you in a fight?"

"Never mind that now, Max. I'll tell you about it later." Sammy turned to Harry Mitchell. "Mr. Mitchell, I'm ready to play. If my name's still on the roster, that is."

"It's there. You can pinch hit for Jansen. Maybe you can spoil Goslin's bid for a no-hitter."

Sammy was anxious to get into the game. He'd had an eventful day at Tumbling Waters. He'd tell Max and Marty about it later. Now it was time to have some fun.

Facing the baffling knuckleballs of Goslin, Sammy waited patiently for the pitcher to make a throwing mistake. And Goslin did. Perhaps his success began to go to his head because he tossed a knuckler straight down the middle, the ball dipping as it neared the plate but not as sharply as others he'd thrown. Sammy timed his swing perfectly. He strode forward and whacked the ball hard. It sailed over second base and into the outfield. The centre fielder charged the ball and almost trapped it in his glove before it hit the grass. But he failed to get there in time. The ball caromed off his leg and rolled deeper into the outfield. By then Sammy, showing great speed, had rounded second. He slid into third before the right fielder, who'd finally chased down the ball, could wheel and throw to the base.

Miller fans leaped to their feet and applauded Sammy's timely hit. A number of Chatsworth fans groaned. Out on the mound, Goslin spit in his glove and then hurled it to the ground.

When the ovation died down, Max stepped up to the plate. Goslin had recovered his poise and grinned in at him.

"I've been saving my best knucklers for you, Mitchell," he taunted Max.

And he threw one that dipped sharply over the plate. Max could see the seams on the ball as he swung and missed by inches. It was like trying to hit a bumblebee.

"Har, har," laughed Goslin.

His next pitch soared high, then dropped like a stone. It would have struck the plate if Max hadn't swung his bat. He missed, this time by a foot.

"Har, har, har," roared Goslin.

His laugh was infectious and many of the fans chuckled along with him. It appeared to everyone that his pitches were unhittable. Sammy Fox must have been the luckiest guy in baseball to make contact with one.

Max was embarrassed. He had a reputation as a dangerous hitter and Goslin was making him look foolish. He would have to adjust to those tantalizing knuckle balls. But how? Sammy Fox had stepped forward, moving into the ball to nail his double. Had it been a fluke hit or...?

Goslin wasted no time. He was having fun teasing Max with his fluttering pitches. Now he unleashed another one. The ball floated in, spinning lazily, then fell like a punctured balloon. Teeth clenched, Max took a long stride forward and lashed into it with his bat.

He fully expected to miss but his keen eyes followed the flight of the ball until it collided with his heavy Louisville Slugger. His powerful upper body followed through and he muscled the ball high in the air. *A harmless high fly*, he thought at first. *No, it's more than that*, he thought again. *It's got a chance.*

The ball flew high over the second baseman, carried out over the head of the centre fielder who was charging back, carried over the chain link fence bordering the field. The centre fielder reached out for it, his glove extended. But he slammed into the barrier and tumbled back as the ball flew over the fence.

A home run!

Sammy Fox scampered home from third and waited for Max to circle the bases. Miller fans were jumping in joy.

Sammy and his mates pounded Max on his back when he crossed the plate. His dad said, "Great hit, son." And Marty added, "You sure knocked that silly grin off Goslin's face."

Breathing hard, Max said, "Take it easy, fellows. Game's not over."

But Max had renewed confidence now. And he'd just taken the wind out of Goslin's sails. He fanned the side in the eighth and entered the bottom of the ninth nursing a one-run lead. A bad call by the umpire on what looked like a third strike allowed the leadoff batter to walk to first. When he tried to steal second Marty picked him off with a big league throw to the base. One out.

The next batter fouled several pitches off. Max finally retired him with a fastball that rocketed into Marty's big mitt.

Goose Goslin stepped in—a tough out.

"Gimme yer best pitch, Mitchell," he demanded. "I'll send it to the moon."

But Max pitched Goslin carefully, hitting the inside corner for two strikes, then missing the same corner for two balls. With the count 2–2, Goslin swung wildly at a fastball and got the end of his bat on it. The ball trickled slowly down the third base and stayed fair. Goslin scampered into first with a single.

There he jeered at Max, hoping to upset him.

"Yer all washed up, Mitchell," he brayed. "Lost your fastball and lost yer nerve. Watch my dust. I'm going to steal second on you."

It was the boast that did it. Max waved for Marty to join him on the mound. And he waved Sammy in to hear his plan.

"I'm certain I can get this next batter out," he said. "But I'd rather make Goslin the goat of the game. It'll be fun."

"How you gonna do that?" Marty asked.

"Here's how. Make out like you're mad at me. Wave your arms around. Take a little poke at me. When you do, I'll slip the ball into your glove. We'll try to catch the 'Goose' with the old hidden ball trick."

Marty hid a smile and did as Max suggested.

Goslin applauded the meeting on the mound, especially when he saw Marty poke his brother in the stomach. "Give it up, Marty," he called out. "Yer brother's all outta gas. We've got him on the run. His arm's deader than roadkill."

Goslin watched Marty return to his catcher's position and squat down. Then he eyeballed Max. "Throw it over here, big boy!" he taunted Max. "See if you can pick me off."

Goslin was proud of his speed and he danced off the bag, moving a couple of long strides toward second base—teasing Max. "Come on, busher!" he shouted. "Got you rattled, haven't I? Bet you can't catch me." He stuck out his tongue at Max.

"Bet you we can, you big show-off," Max muttered to himself. He smiled when he saw Goslin take another small step toward second base. Out of the corner of his eye Max saw Marty straighten up and fire a bullet to Sammy Fox, standing on the bag.

"Gotcha!" Sammy exulted, slapping the tag on Goslin, who dove frantically back. Too late!

"Yer OUT!" roared the first base umpire.

"Game over!" shouted the ump at home plate. He turned to pat Marty on the arm. "Nice play, kid. You surprised the heck out of the mouthy kid on first. He was fast asleep on the play. And you know what?"

"What?" said Marty.

"You surprised me, too. I haven't seen the hidden ball play pulled in years. It was fun to watch."

The Millers ran on the field, whooping it up, congratulating Max and Marty for their heads-up play.

Harry Mitchell had mixed emotions after the win. When the excitement died down, he said to Amy, "I'm glad we won the game but I'd rather have seen Max get a strikeout to finish them off. To me, the hidden ball trick borders on cheating."

"But, hon," she replied, "Isn't it all part of the game? How many times have you seen outfielders race in to catch a fly ball and the ball hits the ground just before it pops into their glove. They pretend they caught it and if the umpire is fooled, they're delighted. Or the player who slides into a base and kicks the ball out of an infielder's hands. Is that cheating or is it just baseball?"

"Good point," Harry said. "Old Ty Cobb was a master at that. He broke a few fingers in his day. If it's not cheating, it's certainly unsportsmanlike. Players who do those things will tell you, 'No big deal. You do anything to win.' And maybe they're right. Me? I've always believed in fair play. After all, it's just a game. Sometimes it's hard to figure out what's right and what's wrong in sports."

Amy took his arm. She said, "I like the fact you believe in fair play and that you want the boys on the team to think about what's cheating and what isn't. Look at hockey. Players trip each other when the referee has his back turned. They take dives to force a penalty. The goalies wear pads that are wider than the rules allow. That's not fair. But it happens."

Harry smiled. "You're right, of course. Maybe I'm naïve to think that classy players—real sportsmen—don't cheat. Someday Max and Marty will have coaches who'll teach them all the sneaky tricks that might win a game or a pennant. Then they'll have to decide for themselves what to do."

"I'm sure they'll make the right decisions, hon," Amy said, tightening her grip on his arm. "And they'll be lucky if they ever get a coach as smart as you."

CHAPTER 8

THE FRIENDLY RIVALS

"Birds of a feather," Max said to Marty.

"Flock together," Sammy Fox finished the sentence.

The Millers were still celebrating their victory, milling around behind the team bench, enjoying soft drinks and talking about their win over the Cougars.

Across the deserted diamond, the Cougars were standing near their team bus, getting ready to make the return trip to Chatsworth.

"Hey! What's Darrel Dugan doing over there?" Marty exclaimed. "He's talking to Goose Goslin like they're old buddies."

"Maybe they are," Sammy Fox said. "They both like to bend the rules."

"And they both think they're MVPs," said Marty, taking a swig from his bottle.

"That's what Sammy and I meant," Max said. "When we said birds of a feather flock together."

"I get it," Marty said. "I'm not dumb. Neither one of those guys is very popular, right? They both have a mean streak and, oh, I don't know, they seem to think they're better than anybody else. They're just not very nice to be around."

The Chatsworth players filed onto the bus. They had an hour's drive ahead of them. Before he boarded, Goslin pointed at Max and sneered, "I'll get you next time, Mitchell. Nobody makes a fool out of me and gets away with it."

Max didn't bother to answer. But Marty put his hands to his mouth, pulled his lips back and stuck out his tongue at Goslin.

Darrel Dugan came shuffling across the infield and flopped down next to his teammates.

"What was that all about, Darrel?" Max asked. "I didn't know you were pals with Goslin."

"We're not pals," said Darrel testily. "We got some common interests, is all. Baseball cards and things. Nothin' wrong with talking to an opposing player is there?"

"I guess not," said Max. "It's just that most of us have no use for Goslin and his ways."

"Aw, he's not so bad," declared Darrell. Changing the subject, he asked Sammy, "How come you were late today? You let us down, pal. And where'd you get all those bumps and bruises?"

Sammy said bitterly, "I was riding Annabelle to

the game when some kids in a jalopy raced by me on the road. They blasted the horn and Annabelle bolted. She threw me into some bushes. The kids laughed and one of them hollered, 'Another red-skin bites the dust.' And that's why I missed most of the game."

"Hmm," said Darrel. "Why don't you tell my Dad? Maybe he could pick them up. Talk some sense into them."

Sammy shrugged. "I can't imagine your dad being interested in my problems," he answered.

Darrel didn't appear to be much interested, either.

"Sure, sure," he said, stifling a yawn. "Well, I'm going home. Got lots of things to do besides sit and talk about a harmless prank."

Harmless prank? Sammy bristled and started to his feet. But Max put a hand on his arm and he sat back down. Darrel walked toward a freshly painted yellow car parked under the trees. He turned and delivered a parting shot, "Sammy, I'm glad you live on the reserve with your people and I live in town with mine. That way we get along just fine." He chuckled.

Once again, Sammy started to rise and Max held him back.

"Hey, Darrel," shouted Marty. "Where'd you get the car?"

"I bought it yesterday. It's a beaut, isn't it? I'll give you a ride in it someday soon."

The car was a few years old but spotless.

"How much did you pay for it?" Marty asked brashly.

"Hundred bucks," replied Darrel. "I sold some of my best baseball cards. Got 20 bucks for my Ty Cobb card alone."

When he drove off, Marty said, "Lucky guy. Imagine buying a car with baseball cards."

Max said, "That car looks like it's worth a lot more than 100 bucks. His dad must have chipped in. Darrel doesn't have a part-time job, does he?"

"Not that I know of," said Marty.

"That bum?" Sammy said bitterly. "He's too lazy to work." Sammy was still fuming.

"He's got some nerve," Marty snorted when Darrel drove off. "Talking to you like that, Sammy."

"That's right," Max agreed. "He's a good ballplayer, but a mouthy one. Oh well, a team is made up of all kinds of players. Some players put the team first and never quit; others think only of themselves and their stats. Some are good sports; others are poor sports."

"That's what a team is," Sammy added. "A bunch of guys or girls thrown together. Some are leaders, some are followers, but all try to play together to win something."

"What kind of team player do you think I am, Max?" Marty asked, fishing for a compliment.

"Funny you should ask," his brother replied. "Sammy and I were just picking out a nickname for you, a name that best describes your role."

Marty beamed. "And what did you come up with?"

"Well, we couldn't decide between 'Lazybones' Mitchell or 'Gabby' Mitchell."

"Or 'Fumbles' Mitchell," Sammy added.

Sammy had to move fast to avoid the big catcher's mitt Marty hurled at his head.

CHAPTER 9

AT THE HOSPITAL

The Mitchell brothers were sitting in two straight-back chairs in Mrs. Anderson's hospital room. Max had picked some flowers from his mother's garden and had put them in a vase. One of the nurses pushed them this way and that to enhance their beauty.

"Aren't they lovely?" she said, before scurrying off.

Marty placed a brown paper bag on the nightstand.

"What did you bring?" asked Max. "What's in the bag?"

"Chocolates. A box of chocolates."

Max frowned. "Mrs. Anderson is still in a coma. How's she going to eat chocolates?"

"They'll be there for her when she wakes up," Marty whispered. "And she'll probably insist that we have some."

"What kind of chocolates did you bring her?"

"Chewy ones. And some real hard ones."

Max rolled his eyes. "You've seen Mrs. Anderson. You know she doesn't have all her teeth."

"Why are we here, anyway?" Marty said.

"Mom talked to the doctor. He said Mrs. Anderson showed signs of regaining consciousness. She may come out of her coma at any minute. He said it would be good if someone was in the room when she does."

"Well, she'll be glad to see you, Max. You saved her life."

Mrs. Anderson stirred under her blanket. She uttered a long sigh.

"That's a good sign," Marty whispered. "She may be waking up."

Max leaned in close to Mrs. Anderson. He saw her eyelids flicker. Heard her moan quietly.

"I thinks she is waking up," he whispered to Marty. "Perhaps you should run and tell the nurse."

Marty rushed from the room.

Slowly, Mrs. Anderson turned her head toward Max. She reached out from under the blanket and took his hand.

"Where am I? Am I in—in the hospital?" she murmured, looking around. Her eyes were open. Her grip on Max became stronger.

"Yes, you are, Mrs. Anderson," Max said. "You've been asleep for a long time. My brother is getting the nurse."

"You're Max," she said, trying to smile. "Max Mitchell. It's so nice to see you again. Did you bring me those nice flowers?"

"Yes, I did, Mrs. Anderson. And my brother Marty brought you some—well, he brought you a little gift, too."

"How sweet of you both."

A frightened look passed over Mrs. Anderson's face.

"What happened to me, Max? Why am I here?" She took another deep sigh.

Max wasn't sure what to tell her.

"You fell, I believe," he said. "You hit your head."

"I remember now," Mrs. Anderson said, her voice barely a whisper. "Two men—caught them in my house—surprised them—robbing me. No lights on. I screamed and ran. They chased me down the path. It was very dark and I fell. I screamed again..."

"You fell into a gully, Mrs. Anderson. Or were pushed. We found you there. Do you recall the sheriff coming to help you? He told us you were conscious for a few moments."

"Yes, yes, Sheriff Dugan helped me. I remember that. Then everything went black."

"The sheriff wanted to know if you recognized the robbers. He said you spoke to him briefly."

"Well, I think I did speak to him, if he said so. But I don't remember much of what I said."

She coughed and Max reached for a glass of water on her bedside table. She took a sip and he put it back.

"The sheriff said you identified the robbers. You said, 'two darkies chased me.' "

Mrs. Anderson's eyes grew wide. She frowned. "No, Max, he got it wrong. I didn't say, 'two darkies chased me'; I said, 'it was too dark to see.' I don't know who was in my house. They wore caps —those floppy peaked caps."

Max sat upright. If Mrs. Anderson had said, "two darkies chased me," then Josh and Satch were in deep trouble. But if she'd said, "it was too dark to see," it made a world of difference. And he'd never seen Satch or Josh wearing peaked caps.

"Young men or old, Mrs. Anderson?"

"Hmm. Not sure. But I would guess young." She frowned, thinking hard now. "Max, there may have been three of them. I heard them talking about meeting a redhead later. At least I think they said redhead. My hearing isn't what it used to be."

"A redhead? That's a surprise. There aren't many redheads in Indian River."

"There's the O'Brien twins," Mrs. Anderson stated. "They've got red hair."

"That's true, Mrs. Anderson," Max agreed. "But the O'Brien twins are only ten years old."

She smiled weakly. "The O'Brien twins are little devils but I don't think they go around robbing old ladies like me."

Mrs. Anderson put her hands to her face. Tears trickled down her cheeks.

"What's wrong, Mrs. Anderson?" Max asked. "Please don't cry."

Her words were muffled and Max could barely hear them.

"I've lost everything," she sobbed. "My money, what little jewellery I owned. All gone. My house in ruins. And I've got no insurance—no husband to look after me. I'm destined for—for the poorhouse."

Max squirmed in his chair, not knowing how to comfort her. "It's okay, Mrs. Anderson. We'll think of something."

She stopped crying, and nodded. She put on a brave smile. "Maybe you're right. Thank you, Max."

The door flew open and a nurse rushed in, followed by a doctor. Marty was close behind. The doctor examined Mrs. Anderson. He seemed pleased with the results.

"Everything is looking good," the doctor pronounced. "Very good. Now, is there anything we can get you, Mrs. Anderson? How about something to eat?"

"I brought you some chocolates, Mrs. Anderson," Marty piped up.

She gave Marty a grateful smile. "That was sweet of you, Marty. You help yourself. Take as many as you want. I think I'll settle for a bowl of soup."

Marty didn't need any further encouragement. He took a handful of the chewy ones and shoved them in his pocket.

On the way home, it began to rain hard. The boys took shelter under a tree next to the road. "What about lightning, Max?" Marty asked, looking skyward. "We shouldn't be under a tree."

Max said, "It's just a downpour, Marty. No thunder. No lightning. We'll be okay here."

He told Marty about his brief conversation with Mrs. Anderson.

"I just hope she tells the sheriff what she told me," he said. "Sheriff Dugan thought she said, 'two darkies chased me.' He assumed she meant Satch and Josh."

"Maybe that's what he wanted her to say," Marty suggested. "Maybe he should get his ears cleaned out."

"I wonder if those rowdy kids that Sammy mentioned could have robbed her," Max said. "They may have been in town that night. They could have been wearing caps. You know, as a disguise."

"Can't think of anyone else who might have done it," Marty said. "Whoever did it should go to jail. And for a good long time. Mrs. Anderson

88

almost died. And now you say she may wind up in the poorhouse."

"She said something odd, Marty, while you were out of the room. She told me there might have been a third person involved. She said she heard the two robbers talking about meeting later—at a redhead's."

"Hmm. Can't think of any red-haired kids in town—except for me." Marty ran a hand through his hair.

Max chuckled. "You've got reddish brown hair, Marty. Sure there's some red in it but I'd hardly call you a pure redhead. But if you want to be considered a suspect..."

"No, no," Marty said quickly. "You're right. I'm no redhead."

"We'll go visit her again in a day or two. And maybe we could go over and cut her grass for her."

"I'll bring her some more chocolates," Marty said, grinning. Just then he remembered the chocolates he'd stuffed in his pockets. "Oh oh," he said, reaching for them. His fingers encountered chocolaty goo. "Mom just washed these pants," he said.

Max gave his brother a frosty look.

"You'd better wash them under the hose when we get home," he said. "And don't be shaking hands with anybody."

The rain began to let up and they walked on.

In the distance, a car raced down the street toward them, coming fast. Max and Marty moved back from the curb but not quickly enough. The car hit a deep puddle in the road and sheets of water flew out from the spinning wheels. Max and Marty were splashed with the muddy slop.

"Hey!" shouted Marty. "That fool soaked us. Those rowdy kids again?"

"That fool was Darrel Dugan," Max growled, wiping mud from his face. "In his yellow car. He's going somewhere in a hurry. He's headed out of town."

"I hope he crashes," snorted Marty. "I guess he thinks he can drive like a maniac. Who's going to stop him—his father?"

"He soaked us on purpose," said Max angrily. Then he shrugged. "Oh, well. Let's get home and get out of these clothes. Now we'll both be washing under the hose."

CHAPTER 10

SOLVING A MYSTERY

Later in the day, wearing freshly ironed pants and shirts, the Mitchell brothers shared a booth at Merry Mabel's with Trudy Reeves and her friend Sandy Hope.

They had received a rude greeting from Mabel when they arrived.

"I see those friends of yours are in jail," she said. "I hear they tried to murder poor old Mrs. Anderson. We don't need their kind in town."

"We don't think they did it," Max said defensively. "Nobody saw them do it."

"Ha!" snorted Mabel. "I took one look at them and knew they were troublemakers. I guess the sheriff knew it too. You boys should be more careful of the company you keep."

Max and Marty decided it wouldn't do much good to argue so they proceeded to the booth. They ordered ice cream.

It had barely been served when Sandy passed a paper napkin to Marty. "Better wipe that ice cream off your clean shirt," she suggested. "Chocolate ice cream on a white shirt really stands out."

"First time that's ever happened," Marty said, grinning. He wiped a glob of ice cream off his shirt. "I'm known for my impeccable table manners."

"Sure you are," Max said. "You should see my brother eat peas off a knife."

They were discussing Mrs. Anderson, and both girls were delighted to hear she was well on her way to recovery.

"But we can't figure out what she meant about meeting at a redhead's," Max said. "Know any troublemakers in town with red hair?"

Trudy said, "A couple of girls in school have red hair. But they're not troublemakers. No boys I can think of. Wait a second. Mrs. Anderson doesn't hear well, does she? I wonder if she confused the word 'redhead' with something else. Like red bed. Or red shed. You know, a place where robbers might hide their loot. Is there a red shed in Indian River?"

"There might be," Max said. "Although I can't think of one."

"Most sheds are unpainted," said Sandy. "Most are weathered boards, aren't they? Like barnboard?"

"We could drive around and look for sheds," Marty suggested. "It doesn't take long to drive around a place like Indian River."

"I've got my dad's car for the day," Trudy said. "Let's go."

The four teenagers drove up and down the streets of Indian River, peering out the car windows, looking for sheds. They saw a number of them but none was painted red.

They drove around the outskirts of town with no better luck.

"Heck, we're halfway to Chatsworth," Marty said. "Why not drive out that way? We can stop at the cheese factory. There's an ice cream store next door."

"You and your ice cream," Max sighed. "There's already enough left on your shirt to last you a week."

"We'll do it," Trudy said, accelerating. "Just point me in the right direction."

They were almost to the cheese factory when Sandy shrieked. "Stop! Stop! There's a red shed," she exclaimed. "Back there. Tucked in among the tall grass and trees. I was lucky to see it. Turn around, Trudy."

Trudy obeyed and within moments she had turned into a bumpy lane that led through a field of hay into the woods. On each side of the path, tall maple trees towered over them. Just ahead was a tumbledown shed painted red.

"It's a maple syrup shack," Max said. "And it looks deserted."

"Nobody taps the trees in these woods," said Sandy. "Not anymore. My dad knows the owner of this land. He's in the old folks' home—too old to make syrup."

Trudy drove up to the shed and parked in the tall grass behind some shrubs. The windows in the shed were boarded over.

"There are fresh tire marks near the door," she observed. "Somebody's been here. And not too long ago."

He noticed some writing scrawled on the door. KEEP OUT! THIS MEANS YOU!

Max hesitated for a moment. "Let's take a look," he said. He got out of the car, marched boldly up to the shed and pushed against the door. It flew open and Max gasped.

"Look!" he called out. "Look what's in here!"

The others gawked when they looked inside.

"Holy smoke!" said Marty. "It's filled with all kinds of stuff. You go in, Max. We'll wait here."

Max entered the shed. A mouse scurried away, seeking a hiding place. He brushed a spider's web from his face. To his right, on the floor, was an old burlap bag. He picked it up and looked inside. Nothing. But underneath the bag was a mahogany box. *It's like the one Mom has on her dresser at home*, Max thought, *only bigger*. He picked up the box and opened it. Jewellery! And lots of it. "Looks expensive," he murmured. He noticed two other wooden boxes nearby and opened them. A silver table setting was in one and someone's coin collection in another.

"Wow!" he called out to his friends. "Lots of valuable stuff in here. But what's it doing in an unlocked shed—in the woods?"

He turned to leave when he stumbled over another box. He stopped to open it.

Cash! At least 300 or 400 dollars in bills. Mostly fives and tens.

"Marty, look here," he called out. "There's a lot of money in this box. Who would be foolish enough to leave all this cash in an old shed—with no lock on the door?"

"Lock or no lock it makes no sense," Marty said after he examined the contents of the box. "Anybody could walk off with it."

Trudy spoke up. "I think all this stuff is stolen property. That's what I think."

"Even the money?" Sandy asked. "But Max was right. Who would leave money lying around like this?"

"Somebody who was confident enough to think it was safe here," Trudy replied. "Confident that no one would ever come poking around this old shed."

"And someone who didn't want to be seen carrying a lot of cash around," Marty suggested.

"Someone who would arouse suspicion by putting that much money in a bank."

"Let's get out of here," Max said. "If a gang of thieves left this stash here they may come back. We don't want to be here when they do."

In the distance they could hear the whine of an engine. A vehicle was coming and it slowed as it approached the entrance to the field.

"Oh oh," Marty said. "It may be too late. Quick! Get down in the long grass."

They kneeled in the grass. Max peeked through an opening and saw a green truck slowly turn down the trail that led to the shed.

The truck stopped. Two large, rough-looking men got out.

"We may be in trouble," Max whispered. "Looks like one of them is carrying a rifle. If they're the thieves…"

Then a look of relief crossed his face. He smiled.

Marty pulled on his pant leg. "What's so funny?" he whispered. "We should run for it."

"Relax, brother," whispered Max. "What looked like a man with a rifle is a man with a shovel over his shoulder. They're going back to the road and filling in a pothole. They're a repair crew for the county roads. They'll be finished in a few minutes. Then we can leave. But I don't mind saying they had me scared for a minute."

CHAPTER 11

SETTING A TRAP

The photo of Sandy Hope on the front page of the *Indian River Review* failed to hide her freckles—or her braces—but it captured her impish smile. And it certainly caught the attention of the paper's subscribers.

"She looks adorable," Amy Mitchell said. "I love the way she's kissing that baseball. Marty, you're turning out to be a great photographer."

"Thanks, Mom," Marty said. "Dad said he'd put my photo of Sandy in the paper if it would help us catch the guys who've been breaking into places and robbing people in town."

"And how is Sandy's photo going to help?"

Max joined the conversation. "Sandy owns a fabulous baseball with Babe Ruth's signature on it. And a lot of valuable baseball cards. So we figured we'd put her collection on display tomorrow—at the community centre. In a showcase there. People can come to see it free of charge."

"I still don't see how that's going to help you catch some petty thieves."

"Mom, we think the robbers are interested in old sports stuff," Max explained. "Some of it's really valuable. They'll see the story about Sandy and maybe come to the community centre and try to steal her collection. We'll be hiding out there and find out who they are. If they try to break into the showcase, Marty will take their photo. It'll help prove that Satch and Josh didn't steal anything."

"That sounds too dangerous to me," their mother said. "Why doesn't Sheriff Dugan do the hiding?"

"He's out of town, Mom. At some golf tournament in the city. Dad tried to reach him to tell him about the shed full of loot we found. He hasn't called back yet. Then Dad called Billy Calhoon, his deputy. Billy said that with the sheriff away, he was too busy to look into it today. He said to call back tomorrow. I think Dad woke him up."

"Well, somebody should investigate," their mother said. "If the sheriff doesn't call back, and Billy Calhoon is too lazy to get off his backside, perhaps your father and I should drive out to this shed you mentioned."

"Great idea, Mom," Max said. "We can show you where it is. We can do it tomorrow—after we're through at the community centre."

"We can even slap a padlock on the shed door," Marty suggested.

Mrs. Mitchell still didn't like the idea of her sons playing detective. "No adult supervision at the community centre, no deal," she said.

"But Dan Jenkins, the manager of the community centre, will be there. He promised to help," Marty pleaded.

"Hmm. Well, I guess that might be all right," she said, relenting. "Dan Jenkins is as strong as an ox. And he's as responsible as a judge. What time will you be home?"

"Community centre closes at six o'clock. Right after that."

"All right then," she said. "But be careful. And if the thieves do show up, just take photos. No confrontations. Let Dan Jenkins take care of things. And if they don't show up and the sheriff hasn't called, we'll all drive out to the shed."

———

In the dank basement of an old house many blocks away, two conspirators huddled over a small table. They were smoking cigarettes and reading a newspaper under the glow of a small lamp they'd plugged into a socket in the wall.

"We make a great team, don't we?" one of the conspirators said. "We've already ripped off a dozen people in town and stashed away hundreds of dollars in cash and jewellery and other stuff."

"Yep," nodded his accomplice. "And if anybody is under suspicion it's those two ball players who came to town...Paige and Gibson."

"I think we should give ourselves glamorous nicknames," suggested the first conspirator. "I'll be John Dillinger and you can be Al Capone. They're about the most famous criminals I know. They're great role models."

"All right!"

The young men shook hands.

"Nice to meet you, John Dillinger."

"Likewise, Mr. Capone."

"You can call me J.D. for short."

"And you can call me Al."

J.D. poked his finger at the front page of the newspaper. "Look at this. That little tomboy, Sandy Hope, has her Babe Ruth baseball on display. And a lot of valuable baseball cards as well."

"I'd love to get my hands on them," Al said. "We could sell them to a guy in the city who'd pay big bucks for that kind of stuff."

They scanned the write-up under the photo of Sandy Hope.

"Why, her collection is in the community centre—in a showcase," J.D. said. "With only Dan Jenkins to look after it."

"That old fart," snorted Al. "We can fool him easy. Late this afternoon, when everybody goes home for dinner, we'll go over there. I'll crawl around through the bushes behind the hall. I'll sneak in the back door and cause a distraction while you crack open the showcase and grab the baseball and the cards."

"What kind of a distraction?" asked J.D.

"There's a kitchen attached to the hall," Al said, smiling wickedly. "I'll fill a pop bottle with gasoline, attach a fuse to it, light it up, throw it in the door and bingo! A big fire in the kitchen should bring Jenkins running. Anyone else in the building will run for the exits. That's when you walk in the front door, crack open the showcase, throw the stuff in your sports bag and get out of there. You'll be in and out in 20 seconds. I'll be waiting around the corner in my car."

J.D. nodded his head approvingly. "A great plan," he said. "It'll be exciting to pull off a stunt like this. That dope Jenkins will be totally confused."

The plan worked to perfection. Shortly before six o'clock, a few stragglers left the building. It was time for dinner. The community centre was deserted except for the presence of Max, Marty and Dan Jenkins, who were hiding behind a screen off to one side. Marty had his camera trained on the showcase, its lens poking through a crack in the screen.

Suddenly they heard a loud explosion. It came from the rear of the building. They jumped up to see flames leaping out of the door leading to the kitchen.

"Fire extinguisher!" shouted Jenkins, racing to an alcove and yanking a heavy cylinder off the wall. "Come on, help me, fellows!"

The Mitchells and Jenkins ran to the rear of the hall. They passed a bathroom and Jenkins shouted, "There's a bucket in there. Fill it up!"

The Mitchells found the bucket and filled it with water from the tap. They dashed toward the flames and doused them with water. Jenkins wielded the fire extinguisher and sprayed foam around the kitchen until there was nothing but smoke in the room.

They retreated slowly, making certain the fire was out.

"Wow! That was close!" exclaimed Jenkins, resting the fire extinguisher on the floor. "But how did it happen? There was nobody in here."

Max said, "There must be a reason for it. Fires don't just light themselves."

They washed their hands in the bathroom and moved back into the main hall. They were approaching their hideaway behind the screen when Marty grabbed Max by the arm.

"Look!" he cried out. "The showcase is broken. There's glass all over! Sandy's collection is gone!"

———————

Sandy Hope was distraught when she learned her prized baseball collection had been stolen. Max and Marty went to her house to deliver the bad news.

"My parents warned me," she said. "Not to advertise I owned such valuable items. They told me not to trust anyone. But I trusted you, Max and Marty. Now look what's happened." Sandy burst into tears.

"We're really sorry, Sandy," Max said. "You see, there was a fire and..."

"Oh, I don't want to hear about it," Sandy blubbered. "Leave me alone. I just want my things back."

When Max called Sandy an hour later, her mother answered the phone.

"Sandy's not here, Max," she said. "She and Trudy rode off on their bicycles some time ago. She said she had a hunch where she might find her precious collection. She was pretty upset..."

Max asked Mrs. Hope to call him the moment Sandy returned. He called Trudy's house and talked to Mrs. Reeves.

"I don't know where she went," Trudy's mother said. "She said something about meeting Sandy."

CHAPTER 12

CAPTURED BY THIEVES

Sandy tentatively pushed open the door of the red shed. She heard a sound.

"Just a mouse," Trudy said. "Don't be so squeamish."

She held up her flashlight and moved into the shack.

"Close the door behind you," she instructed Sandy. "We don't want to be seen."

"It smells in here," Sandy said, sniffing. "Let's find my stuff and get on home."

Trudy ran a beam of light around the confines of the shed. There was no sign of a baseball or a collection of cards.

"Nothing here but the stuff we saw before," she muttered.

"Guess my hunch was wrong," Sandy sighed. "I was sure they would be here."

Trudy shivered. "It's creepy in here," she said, looking up. "And I hear rain on the roof. Let's go home. It's almost pitch dark. And there's a storm coming."

Trudy felt something crawl across her foot and yelped.

"A mouse!" she cried out. She reached down to swat it and dropped her flashlight. It fell through a broken floorboard and rolled under the shed.

"Darn it," she muttered.

"Never mind it," Sandy said. "Let's go home."

They stepped out of the shed into the gloom of the night. A bolt of yellow lightning lit up the landscape. A strong breeze rustling the leaves in the trees failed to muffle the sound of a thunderclap that followed, startling them. Trudy shouted, "That was close. I'm afraid of lightning. I think it struck a tree."

They groped on the ground until they found their bikes. The wind swirled through the nearby bushes and the rain splattered their faces. It pounded on the roof of the shed. Another flash of lightning lit up the sky.

Trudy was about to mount her bike when she heard a piercing scream.

"Sandy? What is it?"

Trudy turned toward her friend but a rough hand suddenly covered her face and mouth. Another hand yanked on her hair and she tumbled to the ground. Her bike went flying. A heavy weight fell on top of her, knocking her breathless. Her face was pushed into a muddy pool of water.

Someone had rushed from the bushes and tackled her. She realized that someone else had surprised Sandy in the same manner. Both girls lay on the ground on their stomachs, straddled by two large men. Trudy and Sandy were all but paralyzed by fear.

Their hands were yanked from under their bodies and pulled sharply behind their backs. They grunted in pain as lengths of cord encircled their wrists, binding them tightly.

"Don't you dare scream and don't look back!" warned one of their attackers.

"We'll have to kill you if you do," snarled the other one. "So keep your eyes closed."

Rough hands pulled the girls to their feet. "Walk over to the shed!" ordered Trudy's assailant. "Both of you. Now, move!"

"And don't dare turn and sneak a look at us," repeated the man holding Sandy by the neck.

The two girls obediently shuffled slowly in the direction of the shed. Before they were roughly pushed inside, more cord was wrapped around their ankles and knotted. And both girls were gagged with a dirty piece of cloth tied tightly behind their necks. They heard the snap of a padlock after the door slammed shut. They lay on the wooden floor, shivering with fear and in shock from the suddenness of the attack. They were stunned by the realization that they were far from home, held captive in a smelly shack set far back from the road. It was late on a stormy night and not a single family member or friend knew where they were.

Outside the red shed, Al Capone and John Dillinger huddled and talked in whispers. They had been approaching the shed when they saw movement inside and a flash of light. Then they almost stumbled over the girls' bicycles laying in the grass. It was Dillinger who crept up to the shed and heard the girls talking. He made the decision to capture them before they could rush back to town and report the discovery of stolen goods. He slipped back to the car and retrieved a length of cord from the trunk. He severed it in long pieces with his jackknife. It was he who suggested tackling the girls when they left the shed.

"It's dark. It's beginning to rain," he reasoned. "They won't see our faces if we do this right."

When Al Capone hesitated, stating, "This is serious business. It's like kidnapping. It's assault. We could go to jail for a long time..." Dillinger had taken him by the shirt and shaken him.

"You want to be a big-time criminal, you've got to deal with situations like this," he snarled.

"Somehow those girls discovered our hideout. We've got to subdue them and make sure they don't recognize us."

"Then what?" whined Capone.

"Then we clean everything out of the shed. It'll take a couple of trips to load the trunk of the car. We'll move everything from the red shed to the woodshed behind my house—temporarily. Nobody goes in there in the summer. And we'll get rid of the jewellery and other stuff we've stolen. We'll sell it in the city. Soon as possible."

"What about the girls?"

"When we're finished loading the car, we'll come back for them. I've got some ski masks we can wear over our heads. We'll blindfold the girls and take them deep in the woods. They can stay there until somebody finds them. It could take a day or two. Heck, we may even join the search party ourselves."

"You mean we can be bad guys one minute and good guys the next," stated Capone, suddenly convinced the plan was a good one.

"That's right," Dillinger said, flashing a devilish grin. "This is a good test for us—like an initiation. We'll come through it like pros. And someday, when we're running a big criminal organization, we'll laugh about this night. And how nervous we were."

"Hush!" said Capone. "The light went out. The kids are coming out."

"You take the first one," Dillinger instructed. "Tackle her hard from behind. And don't let up on her because she's a girl. Remember, if one of them sees our faces..." He moved a finger along his throat.

"Murder them?" gasped Al Capone. "You sure we want to go that far? That's a hanging offence."

"Do as I say and you won't have to worry about it," Dillinger growled, pushing his partner forward. "Now move!"

CHAPTER 13

TO THE RESCUE

Max had trouble keeping the car on the road. Sheets of rain slid across the windshield and the wipers could not keep the glass clear. He slowed to a crawl.

"Keep your eyes open for the dirt road leading to the red shed," he ordered his brother. "It's narrow and easy to miss."

"There it is!" shouted Marty. "Just ahead."

Max turned the car into the field and drove through the mud and water leading to the red shed.

"Wish we'd brought our raincoats," Marty muttered as he threw open the door and stepped out. He slipped in the mud and fell to his knees.

"Now my pants are ruined," he griped.

"Never mind that," said Max, moving ahead. "Let's see if my hunch was right."

"I don't think Trudy and Sandy are in that old shed," Marty said. "We're going to look like fools when we find they simply went to the movies."

"Hush!" Max said, cautiously approaching the shed. "Give me your flashlight."

He pushed the shed door open. He stepped inside.

The beam of his light swept back and forth.

"There's nothing here!" he gasped. "I can't believe it."

"No jewellery? No cash?" asked Marty, poking his head inside.

"Nothing," Max answered.

The brothers huddled just inside the shed door, standing out of the driving rain.

Max dropped his arm, wondering what to do next. The beam from his flashlight lit up the ground outside the shed.

"Look!" Marty said in surprise. "Those little ruts filled with rainwater! They're bicycle tracks, aren't they?"

"They must be, Marty. I'll bet the girls came here on their bicycles. And it looks like somebody has been slipping and sliding in the mud next to them."

Marty stepped down and waded through the slop, looking for clues.

"Over here, Max. Look at this. There are muddy tracks—tire tracks—leading down the path into the woods. And they look fresh to me."

"Why would anyone drive into the woods on a night like this?" Max asked.

"Don't know," responded Marty with a sigh. "But something tells me we'd better find out."

"Only a fool would drive down this trail in this weather," Max said, examining the deep ruts made by the tires. "Or someone really desperate to get somewhere."

"You mean we have to walk," Marty complained. "I'm soaked to the skin. And I'm cold."

"We're going to walk," said Max. "I have a hunch the driver of the car, whoever he is, will soon turn back. Or get stuck in the mud. We may not have to go far."

They started down the trail, barely able to follow it as it twisted and turned through the trees, trees that provided scant shelter from the streaming wall of rain.

"We were crazy to drive a car in here," snarled Dillinger. "The rain has made this old trail almost impassable."

Al Capone shuddered. "We can't afford to get stuck in the mud," he said nervously. "We've emptied the shed but someone else might know about it and come looking. Let's dump the girls fast and turn back."

Dillinger stopped the car when he found a place wide enough to turn around.

"This is far enough," he said. "Get the girls out of the back seat. Prop them up against that big tree. Somebody will find them sooner or later."

When Al Capone opened the back door and roughly began to pull the girls from the car, Trudy bent her knees, then lashed out with both feet, catching Capone squarely in the stomach.

"Oooph!" he grunted, stumbling back and falling in a muddy puddle.

"You little..." he snarled, regaining his feet and dragging Trudy from the back seat and sliding her roughly through the mud. He propped her against the tree, was tempted for a moment to throttle her on the spot, thought better of it and returned to get Sandy.

"Leave them for the bears or the wolves to find," he said angrily. "Let's get out of here," he said to Dillinger, rubbing his stomach.

Dillinger began driving the car slowly back through the ruts in the trail. The car's headlights flashed against branches thick with leaves whipped by the wind and soaked by the rain. Once he thought he saw light reflecting off a pair of beady eyes caught in the gleam of the lights. *A wolf*, he thought, *or maybe a bear. Some kind of animal.*

Al Capone had seen it too. He shivered. "Maybe we should have left the girls in the shed," he said.

"No," answered Dillinger sharply. "They might have told someone they were going to the shed. Soon folks will be looking for them. Leaving them in the woods was being smart. It gives us some time."

"Serves them right," Capone responded gruffly. "They should have been minding their own business. We're lucky they didn't see our faces."

Suddenly, Dillinger froze at the wheel. His foot hit the brake and the car slid to a stop.

"What is it?" Al Capone shouted in alarm.

"Somebody's coming."

"Impossible!" Capone replied. "We're a mile from nowhere."

"Look! Two guys up ahead. Slogging through the mud. Coming fast."

Al Capone gasped. "It's those dern Mitchell brothers," he said, wiping the fogged-up windshield with his bare hand. "How did they get here?"

The Mitchells broke into a stumbling run when they saw the headlights of the car.

"Be careful!" Max cautioned Marty. "If they're the robbers, they may have guns."

Suddenly, the car doors flew open. Two men sprang from the vehicle, ski masks hiding their faces. One waved a baseball bat he'd grabbed from the back seat. The other brandished a small knife.

"We can't let them live," Dillinger growled. "They'll turn us in. Let's get 'em!"

They rushed the Mitchells who were at a disadvantage. The blinding headlights and the pelting rain affected their vision.

"Look out!" shouted Max.

"What are we going to do?" Marty shouted back.

Max looked around, frantically seeking a weapon. He found a pile of rocks and scooped one up. Dillinger was coming fast, both arms raised above his head, the baseball bat ready to crush Max's skull.

Max hurled the rock like a baseball. It struck Dillinger in the shoulder and he howled in pain. The bat fell at his feet. He bent down to snatch it up when Max sprang at him, barrelling into him like a football linebacker.

"Yiiiiii!" yelled Dillinger, landing hard on his back and sliding through the mud. Max leaped on him, straddling him, reaching for his neck with one hand and pushing his head backwards, twisting it back into the slop. Dillinger breathed in and found himself choking on muddy water. He thought he was drowning. He panicked. All the fight went out of him.

Marty, meanwhile, was battling Capone in the glare of the headlights. Marty danced away from the flashing blade of the knife. He noticed his attacker had trouble finding his footing in the mud and his thrusts with the knife were mostly wild. Still, if Marty should slip and go down, the fight would end in disaster. Out of the corner of his eye, Marty noticed that Max, still astride his opponent, was reaching for the baseball bat. He plucked it from the mud and wielded it in both hands.

Marty edged closer to his brother, hoping to give Max a chance to catch the knife wielding attacker from behind. Suddenly, Max lashed out, nailing Capone with a swing of the heavy bat, striking him hard behind both knees.

Crack!

Capone's legs buckled and he screamed in pain. His knife flew into the bushes. Marty plunged forward and slammed chest-first into his opponent. Capone, still screaming from the pain of Max's blow, fell backwards, writhing in the mud. He began to moan.

"I give up," he blubbered.

Breathing hard, Max and Marty rose slowly to their feet.

"Nice going, brother," Max gasped.

"You too, Max," Marty said, his chest heaving. "Those guys are bigger than we are."

Max put the baseball bat in Marty's hands.

"They try anything, well, you know what to do," he said. "I'm going to look for Trudy and Sandy."

He didn't have far to go. Within seconds, the two girls were caught in the beam of his flashlight. He pulled off the gags and hastily untied the knots in the cord that bound their hands and legs.

He helped the girls to their feet. Both were unsteady and leaned on him for support.

"Thank you, Max," Trudy murmured into his neck. "I think you may have saved our lives tonight." She gave him a long hug and kissed him on his wet cheek.

"My turn," said Sandy, who rewarded him in a similar fashion.

"Come on," Max said, aware that he was blushing. "Let's go help Marty."

They found Marty standing over the captives, waving the bat menacingly, ready to do serious damage with it if either of the thugs made a move to escape.

"I'm glad you're back," Marty said. "Now let's find out who these characters are."

Max and Marty bent down and removed the ski masks.

They were shocked when they recognized the faces revealed in the beam of the headlights.

"Why, it's Darrel Dugan!" Max said, totally surprised.

"And Goose Goslin," echoed Marty. "I can hardly believe it."

Sandy Hope was as shocked as the others. She nudged Darrel in the ribs with her foot.

"Where's my baseball collection?" she demanded. "Where's my Babe Ruth ball?"

He grimaced, then grunted. "In the car. Back seat."

"Just where you're going," Trudy said in a hard voice. "Look what I've got for you boys."

She dangled several lengths of cord in the air, cords that had encircled her wrists and ankles for the past hour.

She grinned. "I think they'll fit you two just fine. See how you like being trussed up like a Thanksgiving turkey."

They heard a shriek from the back seat of the car.

"My Babe Ruth ball!" Sandy cried out. "It's soaking wet! And covered with mud! The signature has washed off! It's ruined!"

She burst into tears.

"How could you?" she shouted at Darrel and Goose. "That ball is—is irreplaceable."

"We were tossing it back and forth," Goose muttered. "Darrel dropped it and it fell in the mud."

"I did not," Darrel declared indignantly. "It was Goose who dropped the ball—in more ways than one."

Sandy was so angry and upset she marched over and gave each youth a swift kick in the pants.

CHAPTER 14

THE CONFESSION

The lights were on at the police station in Indian River. Sheriff Dugan was on the telephone, talking to Harry Mitchell. In a nearby cell, Satchel Paige and Josh Gibson listened to one side of the conversation.

The sheriff was annoyed. He'd been called from his home to handle a missing person's report, called in by the parents of Trudy Reeves and Sandy Hope. Next there'd been a call from Harry Mitchell who was worried because his sons hadn't checked in.

The sheriff barked into the phone. "No, I don't know where to look for them, Harry. Listen. It's not only your sons who've gone missing but two other kids as well. Yep. Trudy Reeves and Sandy Hope. And my own son, Darrel, hasn't come home tonight. But he told me he'd be late. He's a responsible kid. Went to Chatsworth to visit a friend."

He listened for a few seconds, then glanced out the front window and said, "Harry, a car just pulled up in front of the station. Looks like your car but it's covered in mud. Looks like Max is getting out. Oh, boy, he's covered with mud, too. Looks kinda weird, Harry. Now I see another car pulling up behind. Your son Marty and two girls are getting out of the second car. Hey, it's Darrel's new car—the yellow one. But it's mud-covered too. You better grab a bike or call a taxi and come down here, Harry. Your sons have got a lot of explaining to do."

Max, Marty, Trudy and Sandy stood solemnly in the police station, listening to a harangue from Sheriff Dugan. Before he began his lecture, Max and Marty waved to their friends Satch and Josh through the bars of their cell.

"What's the matter with you young people today?" the sheriff growled. "Scaring us all by going missing on a stormy night. Your folks have been worried sick. Why can't you kids act responsibly? It doesn't say much for your upbringing."

"Sheriff Dugan," Max interrupted. "We can explain. But you're not going to like what I have to say."

"Spit it out, Max. Like I keep telling Darrel, you can't go wrong if you're truthful and honest. Still, you'd better come up with a good excuse for your behaviour tonight."

Max became annoyed. "You should be more concerned for Darrel's behaviour," he blurted.

"Darrel! What's Darrel got to do with this?"

"Sir, you better come out to the car. He's trussed up in the back seat. He can tell you himself."

There was an emotional scene outside the police station when Sheriff Dugan saw his son Darrel and Goose Goslin, their hands and legs bound with stout cord.

Harry Mitchell rode up on a bicycle and heard most of the conversation.

"What's the meaning of this, son?" Sheriff Dugan shouted at Darrel, as he wrestled him from the back seat. Max stepped forward and cut the bindings with the knife he'd picked up back in the woods. He also freed Goose Goslin.

"It's the Mitchells' fault," Darrel whined. "We didn't do nothin'. They beat us up and for no reason at all. Hit us with baseball bats."

Sheriff Dugan turned to Max, outraged.

"Is this true?" he demanded.

"Of course it's not true," Max replied testily. Then his voice steadied. "Your son's a liar and a thief. So is Goose Goslin. We found their hide-out—a red shed—where they've been hiding stolen goods. Trudy and Sandy found it too. And it almost cost them their lives."

Trudy and Sandy nodded affirmatively.

"That's right," said Trudy, still furious over the treatment she and Sandy had received. "Darrel and Goose tied us up and left us in the woods. With bears and wolves and who knows what else all around. Max and Marty saved us."

"Max and Marty were attacked by these two—two creatures," Sandy added. "Not the other way around. Now it's up to you to arrest them and throw them in jail. We don't care if Darrel is your son."

"I need more proof before I'll do that," the sheriff sneered defensively. "My son would never do the things you accuse him of—not my Darrel."

"Oh, no?" Marty piped up. "Ask him where he hid the loot after he took it from the shed. It can't be far away."

"And ask him why he stole my Babe Ruth ball and then dropped it in the mud," Sandy said bitterly.

Sheriff Dugan turned to Darrel, who failed to meet his eye.

"Tell me the truth, Darrel," he said. "Have you really been stealing things from people in town?"

Head down, Darrel confessed all.

"It started with Mrs Anderson," he said, as tears rolled down his cheeks. "When I saw the money in her purse, on the day she was almost run over, I figured she must have a lot more at home. Goose and I went to her house and there were no lights on. So we broke in. She surprised us when she came home. She screamed and ran away. We chased after her and somehow she fell and knocked herself out. We went back and robbed her house."

"You left her in that ditch? Possibly dead?"

"Pop, we thought she was dead. We were scared."

"But not scared enough. You two went back to her house and trashed it. You weren't too scared to rob her of her money and jewels." He gave both youths a look of disgust.

"What else have you got to say for yourselves?" he asked Darrel.

"Well, that seemed so easy, Goose here suggested we rob a few other people."

"Liar!" Goose snorted. "That was your idea, not mine, you mutt. Just like it was your idea to pick nicknames for us."

"Nicknames?" Sheriff Dugan said. "What nicknames?"

Darrel looked embarrassed. "He's John Dillinger. I'm Al Capone," he said sheepishly.

"Do you realize how much time you can spend in jail for what you've done?"

"Well, we didn't plan to get caught," Goose Goslin said.

"Small time crooks never plan to get caught," the sheriff sighed.

"Anyway," Darrel continued. "It was just cash and jewellery mainly. Enough for each of us to buy a car."

"You told me you sold your baseball cards to pay for that car," his father muttered. "Go on."

"We knew about this old red shed in the country. It's been abandoned for years. It seemed like a good place to store our loot until we could sell it to a man in the city. Tonight we moved the stuff to another shed—in the Goslin's back yard in Chatsworth—after we caught the girls nosing around."

The sheriff shook his head in disbelief. He turned to the Mitchell brothers and the two girls. "How did you kids discover this red shed?"

"Mrs. Anderson overheard Darrel and Goose talking about it the night they robbed her," Max said. "But she was confused. She thought they mentioned a redhead, not a red shed."

"She also told me that two darkies robbed her," the sheriff stated. He pointed to Josh and Satchel in the jail cell. "I figured it had to be those two."

"No, she didn't say that," Max corrected. "She said, 'It was too dark to see' when you talked to her before she went into a coma."

The sheriff rubbed his chin.

"Well, maybe she did say that," he granted. "I wasn't too sure what she said."

"Sheriff, after what you just heard from Darrel," Sandy said, "Isn't there something you should do?"

"What's that, young lady?"

"First, let Mr. Paige and Mr. Gibson out of that cell. Then put Darrel and Goose in there instead."

Without another word, the sheriff took a key from his pocket and went to the cell where the two ballplayers were standing.

"Sorry, fellows," the sheriff mumbled as the door swung open. "Guess I made a mistake. You're free to go."

"Thank you, Sheriff Dugan," Satchel said agreeably. "No need to apologize."

"We all make mistakes from time to time," Josh added.

Satch and Josh walked straight to the Mitchell brothers, Trudy and Sandy.

"You four kids did a real good thing tonight," Satchel said, shaking hands with each of them. "You kept your faith in us. You proved our innocence. We'll never forget it."

He turned to Sandy. "I'm real sorry they ruined your Babe Ruth ball. I know how much it meant to you."

Sandy murmured, "I'm sorry, too." Tears welled up in her eyes.

"We all better sit down," the sheriff suggested. "I've got some paper work to do. Got to take statements from everybody involved in this crime." He glared at his son. "These are serious charges I'm dealing with. I never thought I'd see the day when I'd have to lock my own son up in a cell. But I'm gonna have to do that tonight."

He sighed and looked at Harry Mitchell. "I suppose this will be on the front page of the *Review*, Harry? There's no way around it?"

"That's right, Sheriff. I'm afraid there's no way around it."

Harry Mitchell pulled a camera from a bag slung over his shoulder. "Marty, I brought your camera. You better take photos of the accused." He nodded at Darrel and Goose. "With the sheriff's permission, of course."

Sheriff Dugan waved his hand. Go ahead.

"And also the innocent," Harry Mitchell added, nodding at Satch and Josh.

"First, I'll take some shots of Trudy and Sandy," Marty said. "They were the real victims tonight. They were kidnapped!"

"First y'all better wipe your faces with a towel from the bathroom," Josh suggested.

"That's right," laughed Satch. "Otherwise, with all that mud on your faces, you'll look darker than Josh and me."

CHAPTER 15

A PITCHING DUEL

A huge crowd turned out at the ballpark to witness the game between the Satchel Paige All Stars and the Indian River Millers. Satch and his mates were back from a three game tour of small towns farther north where they played before capacity crowds and won all three games. Satch pitched in all 27 innings and won by scores of 3–0, 6–1 and 5–0. Fans rewarded him with a standing ovation when he came through with a no-hitter in the third game.

Most of the residents of the small town of Indian River were now aware of the legendary status of the great pitcher—thanks to a lengthy article about him in the local paper.

Max had written the story of Satchel's remarkable career, his mother had used her editing skills to polish it and his father had been so pleased with it he placed it on the front page of the *Review*. Readers were particularly pleased to discover that Satch and his mates promised to turn over a share of the gate receipts to Mrs. Anderson, to help her get back on her feet.

In a previous issue, the front page had been filled with the story of the two daring teenage robbers—Darrel Dugan and Goose Goslin—and how they were in jail awaiting trial on a number of charges including the attempted murder of Trudy Reeves and Sandy Hope.

The lawyer retained to defend the teenagers ridiculed the charges. "Those two kids didn't attempt to murder those girls," protested Stan "Slick" Stickem, of the firm of Sickem, Prickem and Stickem. "Why, they were just playing a game of hide and seek in the woods and them boys got carried away. They were just havin' a little fun, for heaven's sake."

Despite his gift for the gab, "Slick" Stickem figured Darrel and Goose would be convicted. The judge who would decide their fate—Hanging Horace Gaul—was known for the severity of his sentences. Only the fact that Darrel and Goose were teenagers might save them from years locked up in the penitentiary.

"I'm glad Josh and I didn't have to face Judge Gaul in a court of law," Satch said to Max when they renewed acquaintances before the big game. "They'd be building a scaffold in town about now.

People would be here to see a hanging, not a ball game."

"I don't think the judge would have gone that far," replied Max. "After all, Sheriff Dugan didn't have much of a case against you and Josh."

"Wouldn't have mattered," Satch said. "Where I come from, coloured people get hanged all the time. On the flimsiest of evidence. Sometimes, just having black skin is enough."

"Well, nobody's going to harm you today, Satch. Look at the crowd that turned out to see you pitch. You're a real favourite here. You and Josh both."

Satch grinned. "Yeah, now we are," he said. "Last week? That was a different kind of story." He took his last warmup pitch. "Now I'm ready to play ball. You nervous, Max? Facing the great Satchel Paige in front of your hometown fans? I'll take it easy on you if you want."

"Don't you dare," Max replied heatedly. "Your team has won 30 straight ball games. One more win gives you a perfect season. I'll be out to spoil that record. So don't let up on us. Not for a minute."

"I thought you'd say that, Max. I like your attitude. It'll be fun pitching against you today." He chuckled and added, "Remember, my players may be a little rusty after sleepin' on a bus for a couple of nights. They'll want me to bear down. You may lose by a whopping big score."

―――――――――――――

The umpire kneeled down to dust off home plate. He bent over cautiously, not wanting to risk another split in the seam of his trousers. But this time when he leaned over the plate, he farted loudly. Fans in the front row seats heard the explosion and tittered. Marty, standing behind him, pretended to be choking. He danced around holding his throat with one hand and fanning his face with the other. His actions prompted gales of laughter.

The red-faced umpire glared at Marty and then bellowed, "Play ball!"

On the mound, Max rubbed up the baseball. He turned his back to the plate. His infielders and outfielders chirped encouragement and banged their gloves with their fists. All but one. At second base, Sandy Hope stared nervously at the ground. Her arms and legs felt like jelly. Her mouth was so dry she couldn't have spat like the other players—even if she'd wanted to.

Max called Marty to the mound.

"I'm worried about Sandy," he said. "She looks scared to death."

"She is scared to death," Marty answered. "It's the first time we've had a girl on the team and that's only because Darrel is in jail. Remember, Max, you recommended her. You said she'd probably be better than anybody else we could find."

"That's true," Max admitted. "And I told Dad to play her at second base because of her weak arm. If she fields a grounder she can get the ball over to first base. It's a shorter throw than from third to first."

"Hey, brother, it's just a game. If you're worried about Sandy, throw the ball so nobody hits it to her. In fact, why not pitch a no-hitter? Then you're home free."

Max smiled. Marty's chatter relieved him of most of his concerns. Pitch a no-hitter indeed. Against the Satchel Paige All Stars, the greatest ball club he'd ever faced.

"Batter up!" roared the umpire.

Willie Parsons, the All Stars' leadoff batter, liked to bunt his way to first base. Then he could show off his blazing speed, stealing second, often third and sometimes home with quick bursts of energy.

Max threw a fastball on the outside corner of the plate. Bunt!

But the ball was popped up weakly. Max raced in and gloved it. One out.

The next batter popped up to first base and the third struck out on three straight fastballs.

"Good start, young fellow," Satch said approvingly as he went out of his way to pass Max on his way to the mound. "We're just getting warmed up."

Satchel proceeded to dazzle the Millers with an assortment of fastballs and looping curves from the moment he placed his cleated toe on the rubber. He threw his bee ball and his two hump blooper and used his hesitation pitch as one Miller after another walked to the plate, swung three times at thin air and walked back again.

Max, meanwhile, had every reason to be proud of the way he was pitching. He couldn't remember ever having better control of his pitches. His sizzling fastball caught the corners and his changeup had the All Stars guessing. He even struck out Josh Gibson with a high fastball to end the third inning.

"Great pitch, kid," Josh acknowledged as he turned away from the plate, his bat still on his shoulder. "We haven't faced pitching like that all summer."

"Be careful, Max. Don't give Josh another one like that," Satch called from the sidelines. "He'll hit it from here to Kentucky."

"I'll remember," Max shouted back. He made a mental note. Josh likes high fastballs.

By the sixth inning, the fans began to taunt the All Stars. Indian River supporters had come to the game anticipating some stellar pitching from Satchel Paige and some towering home runs from Josh Gibson. They also expected to see the fleet Willie Parsons steal a number of bases. While Paige's pitching had been impressive, the other two had been rendered mute—thanks to Max Mitchell's hummers.

One of the biggest cheers of the afternoon was earned by a wisp of a girl wearing an oversized uniform—skinny Sandy Hope. In the sixth inning, Josh Gibson smashed a ground ball to her right. Sandy dove headfirst for the ball, snagged it in her glove, scrambled to her feet and threw a perfect toss to Sammy Fox at first—just as Gibson's size 12 shoe hit the bag.

"Yer out!" bellowed the ump at first. "Nice play, Sandy!"

Gibson tipped his cap to the second baseman, acknowledging her sparkling play with a sportsmanlike gesture.

Marty trotted to the mound.

"Still worried about her weak arm?" he said, grinning.

"I can't believe she made that play," Max answered.

In the bottom of the inning, Sandy came to the plate, leading off. And lugging a bat that appeared to be bigger than she was. Satchel chuckled and threw two fastballs across the heart of the plate—both for strikes. Sandy appeared to be petrified of the great man's pitches.

He threw another and the big bat suddenly flashed in an arc. Hard wood connected with white leather and the ball was rifled down the third base line. The All Stars third bagger, playing in "because it's a girl" was struck on the shin by the ball, which ricocheted toward the All Stars' bench.

Sandy flew down the line to first base and then stunned the crowd by racing to second. The third baseman, limping now, retrieved the ball and hurled a bullet to second base. But Sandy was already there. She'd arrived standing up and smiling from ear to ear.

"Way to go, Sandy! Way to go, girl!" screamed the crowd.

A runner at second and nobody out!

"Now's our chance," urged coach Harry Mitchell, clapping his hands together. "Somebody drive Sandy home."

"How about putting a base runner in Sandy's place?" someone asked.

"You kidding?" snorted the coach. "Did you see her scamper to second? We've got nobody faster on the bench."

After Marty popped up to the second baseman, Sammy Fox took his licks. He almost drove Sandy home, muscling one of Satch's bee balls high into left field. But the outfielder raced back and made a leaping catch of the ball.

"Another couple of inches and I'd have had me a triple," Sammy moaned when he returned to the bench. "Dern it."

Now it was up to Max.

Satchel winked at him when he stepped to the plate.

"This is when I bear down, Max," he shouted. "I'll be throwing my pitches but you won't be seein' them. They're just a blur to the normal human eye."

"Then we'll call them blur balls," was Max's retort. "I'm ready when you are."

The first two pitches were exactly that—blur balls. Even the umpire whistled "Wow!" when the pitches found the heart of the plate.

Then Satch teased Max with three straight pitches inches off the outside corner of the plate. Max refused to offer at them and all three were called balls.

"I guess you want another blur ball," Satchel called out. "You ready? Here it comes."

He whistled a fastball right down the middle and Max reacted with a muscular swing. His bat connected with a "crack" and the ball reversed direction, sailing high into the outfield and beyond. The centre fielder waved at it as it sailed over the chain link fence bordering the field.

Home run!

Max circled the bases to thunderous applause. A grin was stamped to his face. He'd homered off the best pitcher he'd ever seen. And his team held a 2–0 lead.

When Max crossed home plate his mates mobbed him. They pounded his back and shook his hand. Old-timers in the crowd couldn't remember when they'd seen such excitement at the ballpark.

On the mound, Satchel Paige tipped his cap to Max. He cupped a hand to his mouth and shouted, "Nice hit, kid."

Max shouted back, "Did you lay it in for me? Did you let me have that one?"

Satch said indignantly, "You kidding? With our winning streak on the line? You earned that one, pal. That was my best bee ball. I should have knocked you down with it."

Satch promptly retired the next batter on three blur balls that almost left a trail of smoke in the air.

Max quickly composed himself after his dramatic home run. He kept the All Star batters guessing with a mix of fastballs, looping curves and changeups. The All Stars dug in at the plate, eager to keep their streak alive, anxious to come from behind and take the lead. And with precious few at-bats left in which to do it.

Max threw brilliantly, catching the corners of the plate with fastballs. Two of the All Stars struck out when he changed the speed of his pitches on three and two counts.

In the top of the ninth, Satch walked the first two batters. A loud-mouthed fan brayed, "Yer through for the day. Take a seat, old man."

Satch grinned up at the man. Then he turned and waved his outfielders in. "Sit on the grass behind the mound," he told them. "You've earned a rest."

Obediently, they sat down. One sprawled on his back, folded his glove under his head and pretended to sleep, snoring loudly.

Everyone laughed, including Mr. Loudmouth.

Satch casually returned to work, threw nine straight strikes and retired the side.

A wave of wild applause saluted his performance.

In the bottom of the ninth, Max began to tire. But he forced the leadoff hitter to pop up. Satchel Paige stepped to the plate. There was no smile this time, no wink. Satch was all business with the bat. A proud professional, he was determined to keep his team's winning streak alive with a dramatic comeback against a rank amateur.

"Strike one!" the umpire howled when Max's first pitch came in low. Satch had checked his swing and complained mildly.

"It was low, ump," Satch complained.

"But you went around on it," the umpire declared.

"Strike two!" chirped the umpire as Satch swung and fouled off the next pitch.

"Shoulda had that one," Satch muttered to himself. "Shoulda hit it into the river."

"Strike threeee!" screamed the umpire after Max threw a lighting fast pitch just over the outside corner of the plate.

Satch was stunned. "That was a blur ball," he mumbled. "A doggone blur ball. Just like one of mine."

He staggered away from the plate, shaking his head. He passed Josh Gibson, who was rubbing up a bat in the on-deck circle. "You going blind, Satch?" Josh asked, straight-faced.

"That kid's a wonder," answered Satch. "He doesn't need any more pitching lessons from me."

"Then I'd better teach him a lesson about hitting," Josh said, striding to the plate oozing confidence. "I know exactly what pitch I'll be looking for."

Gimme a high ball, young fellow, he thought, as he dug his cleats into the dirt next to home plate. *Make it high and fast and I'll send it over the river.*

Marty called time out and ran out to the mound, where Max greeted him coolly.

"I know what you're going to say, Marty," he said. "You want me to walk him."

"Absolutely. It's the best thing to do. The only thing."

"But I want to strike him out."

"Then you're crazy," Marty scoffed. "I say you should walk the guy. You need one more out and there's nobody on base. You're pitching a no..."

"Don't say it, Marty. You'll jinx me. I know what I'm doing."

"But he's the best hitter you've ever faced. And you're tired."

"Not too tired to strike him out. Come on, Marty, this is a real challenge. The easy way out would be to walk him."

Marty shrugged. "Okay. It's your funeral. And when Josh homers I'm going to say I told you so."

Max peered in at Josh Gibson, swinging an enormous bat. *He'll be looking for a high ball*, Max thought. *Okay, I'll give him one. But really high.*

Max wound up and threw hard. The ball soared head-high over the plate. Josh licked his lips, tempted to swing, but he wisely held back. The pitch was too high.

Ball one, signalled the umpire.

Another pitch rifled past the batter's ear. Ball two.

Josh smiled and nodded at Max. *Just a little bit lower, my friend*, he thought. *Just a little bit lower and this game is tied.*

On the mound, Max wiped his brow on the sleeve of his shirt. *He wants one a bit lower*, Max told himself. He toed the rubber, wound up and threw hard. The ball sailed low and away, surprising Josh. He took a mighty swing and missed.

"Not that low," grumbled Josh. Marty heard his remark and chuckled through his mask.

Now the kid is throwing low, Josh thought. *He's smart. Well, I can adjust. Another low fastball like that and...*

The next pitch came in high and hard, fooling Josh. He swung and missed. Too late. The ball smacked into Marty's mitt.

"Aaargh," growled Josh, angry with himself.

With the count three balls and two strikes, the fans rose from their seats and began to clamour.

"Strike him out! Strike him out!"

Josh stepped out of the batter's box and gave them a wave. Then he pointed to dead centre field.

"Look! He's telling us he's going to hit a homer," someone shouted. "Over the centre field fence!"

"Hang in there, Max. Make him whiff!" It was the shrill voice of Sandy Hope, drifting over from second base.

Max took a deep breath and shook off Marty's sign for a fastball. Before Marty could flash another sign, Max was into his windup. He released the ball and Josh flexed the huge muscles in his arms and shoulders. He would send this baby a mile.

The ball sailed in, hovering...hovering. Then it dipped suddenly, darting toward the upper portion of the plate.

"High ball," assessed Josh joyfully. "My specialty!"

The Louisville Slugger moved smoothly off his shoulder. It created a huge arc as Josh aimed it squarely at the ball. He anticipated the sound of bat crunching against ball, sending it high and far into the solid blue sky.

He was aghast when he heard the ball thump into Marty's mitt.

"Strike threee!" screamed the umpire, throwing his arm in the air, thumb upraised. "Yer ouuut!"

CHAPTER 16

A FINAL SURPRISE

The fans roared their approval. Marty raced to the mound and lifted Max off his feet. The rest of the Millers followed, hoisting Max to their shoulders. They paraded him around the infield, dancing, laughing, hollering and celebrating. It was their biggest victory ever!

When Max finally found his feet back on the ground, Sandy jumped into his arms, giving him a hug.

"Thank you, Max. Thank you. That was the biggest thrill of my life. Getting to play baseball against Satch and Josh and the All Stars. And I owe it all to you."

By then the All Stars, who'd been waiting patiently for the excitement to subside, lined up to shake hands with the Millers.

The visitors accepted their defeat graciously and were lavish in their praise of the amateurs from Indian River.

Satch borrowed a megaphone from the public address announcer and addressed the fans before they left the grounds.

"Folks, that was a wonderful ball game," he began. "My team has travelled all over North America and we've compiled quite a winning streak as you know."

"But it ended today," someone in the stands shouted good-naturedly.

"It did indeed," Satch agreed. "And mainly because of this great young pitcher at my side—Max Mitchell."

There was a roar from the crowd.

"I can't recall when any pitcher beat us with a no-hitter," Satch continued. "You should be proud of Max and the Millers."

"We are! We are!" a voice called out.

"A couple more things before we go," Satch said. "First, I'm pleased to say that all the profits from today's game are going to help Mrs. Anderson get back on her feet." He waved to Mrs. Anderson, who was sitting in a wheelchair next to the Millers' bench. She wiped her eyes with a lace hankie, then waved the hankie and mouthed the words, "Thank you, Mr. Paige."

"One of the best of the Millers on the field today," Satch continued, "displayed some excellent hitting and fielding—despite the loss this week of a treasured possession—and despite the fact she's a girl!"

Another roar from the crowd.

"Sandy! Sandy! Sandy!"

"Yes, Sandy Hope is the young lady I'm talking about. Come over here, please, Sandy."

Somewhat confused, Sandy Hope approached Satch shyly, wondering why she was being singled out. Satch took her hand and raised it high.

"Sandy lost a baseball a few days ago," Satch announced. "A special baseball. It was autographed by the greatest hitter in the game—Babe Ruth of the New York Yankees."

The fans murmured, almost silent now, wondering why Satch was telling them something everybody in town knew.

"The name on that baseball is gone forever—thanks to a pair of foolish young men. But me and my teammates want Sandy to have a ball to replace it. I called my friend Babe Ruth this week in New York and he sent me by special delivery another ball. It's signed: 'To my friend Sandy Hope from Babe Ruth.'"

Sandy's upper lip began to quiver. She wiped tears from her dusty face. She embraced Satchel Paige after accepting the ball. She held it high and kissed it. She waved to the fans. Her excitement was contagious and the fans began to applaud and cheer.

Sandy ran over and embraced Josh Gibson and this tough man was so moved that he began to cry.

Satch thrust the megaphone to Max. "Say something, pal," he barked.

Max had to clear his throat. Somehow a lump had lodged in it.

"Folks, our win today was sweet but we all know the All Stars would probably whip us nine games out of ten. More than anything, I want you to know how much the Millers appreciate the chance to play against some of the world's best ballplayers. We know many of them should be— and would be—playing major league ball if—well, if things were different. Satch and Josh stayed in our house and were wonderful guests. They taught Marty and me a lot about the great game of baseball. We're sad they're leaving but we sure hope they'll come back someday. How about a final cheer for these great ballplayers?"

These words prompted another prolonged cheer from the crowd.

"Thank you, all," Max said, stepping aside.

At the bench, while the fans scattered, Satch and Josh thanked Harry and Amy Mitchell for their kindness and their hospitality.

"You've got two fine boys there," Satch said, nodding toward Max and Marty, who were busy signing autographs. "But then you already know that."

Harry said softly, "Thank you, Satch. We're proud of them. What a pleasure it's been getting to know you and Josh."

"You must promise to come back again—and soon," Amy Mitchell said.

"It's a promise," said Satch, turning to leave.

He brushed against Dapper Dan, the barber, who wanted to shake his hand.

"Free haircut anytime you're back this way," Dan promised.

"Appreciate it," Satch grunted. He turned away, pretending he hadn't seen the barber's outstretched hand.

Then Mabel Mercer, owner of Merry Mabel's restaurant, pushed her way through the crowd.

"I hope you gentlemen will stop in at my eating establishment before you go," she gushed. "There's a big table near the front. I can hold it for you and Max and Marty."

"That's very kind of you, ma'am," Satch said pleasantly. "But we have another game to play. Tomorrow afternoon. In a town not far from here."

He tipped his baseball cap, winked at the Mitchell brothers and made his way to the team bus, signing autographs every step of the way.

The sun was beginning to set when the Mitchells arrived home. Big Fella came out of his doghouse and scampered over to greet them.

Max and Marty helped their father gather up the baseball gear. They opened the garage door to put it away when Max froze.

"Marty! Dad! What's that?"

"Looks like a new bike to me," Mr. Mitchell said, smiling.

"Yep. Sure looks like it," Marty said. "A new Glider."

Max was stunned. He moved closer. There was a note attached to the handlebars. He read:

Dear Max,

Josh and me thought you might need this. We're real sorry our team bus crushed your bike. You and Marty and your folks have become good friends in a short time and we treasure that friendship. By the way, it's wonderful to discover that young men and women of your generation are beginning to treat people like us as human beings and equals. Perhaps by the end of this century prejudice and discrimination will fade away and become part of our history. By then, or even sooner, kids with dark skin will be welcome in major league dugouts. Heck, I still hope to get a chance myself although I'll be as old as Methuselah when I finally get the call. Keep on pitching, Max. If you set your mind on it, that strong arm of yours could carry you right to the top. I mean it.

Your friend, Satchel Paige

THE REST OF THE STORY

Sandy Hope played another full season for the Millers before she went off to college where she studied sports journalism.

Mrs. Anderson made a full recovery and was hired by Harry Mitchell to work part time in the advertising department at the newspaper.

Darrel Dugan and Goose Goslin were each sentenced by Judge Gaul to five years in the penitentiary.

Sheriff Dugan resigned from his position and retired to a small town in Florida where he took a job as head of security for a small bank.

Satchel Paige and Josh Gibson never returned to Indian River, although they corresponded occasionally with the Mitchell brothers and Sandy Hope.

Satchel became more and more famous over the years.

In 1937 he said, "Let the winner of the World Series play us—a Negro team—in one game at Yankee Stadium and if we don't win, they don't have to pay us."

He added, "Let the fans take a vote. I've been all across North America and I know the vote would be 100 to one for us." The game was never played.

Satch would have to wait 11 more years, until August 20, 1948, before making his long-awaited major league debut with the Cleveland Indians. On that day he became the oldest rookie in baseball. His lifelong dream had come true. Then 41 or 42, he pitched a 1–0 shutout over the Chicago White Sox before 78,382 fans, a night game attendance record that still stands. He compiled a six to one record during the last two months of the season and helped the Cleveland Indians win the World Series.

Paige had hoped to become the first black player in the majors but his debut with the Cleveland Indians in 1948 came a year after infielder Jackie Robinson joined the Brooklyn Dodgers and captured Rookie of the Year honours. "I guess they thought Jackie was on his way up and I was on my way out," Paige told reporters.

In 1965, at age 59, Satchel pitched his final game in the majors, throwing three shutout innings for the Kansas City Athletics. During his major league career, he often relaxed in his own personal rocking chair between innings.

His proudest day in baseball came in 1971 when he was inducted into The Baseball Hall of Fame, the first player elected from the Negro Leagues. He died in June of 1982.

Josh Gibson was the home run champion of the Negro Leagues and was often called "the black Babe Ruth." He never followed his friend Satchel to the major leagues. "Too old," was the verdict.

Fortunately, Sandy Hope took good care of her Babe Ruth baseball. In 2003, a Babe Ruth autographed baseball in mint condition fetched over $30,000 in an auction on the Internet.